Short Stories of Leo Tolstoy

托爾斯泰短篇小說

What Men Live by・人靠什麼活下去
Ivan the Fool・傻子伊凡

Original Author Lev Nikolayevich Tolstoy
Adaptor Brian J. Stuart
Illustrator Ekaterina Andreeva

WORDS
600

MP3

Let's Enjoy Masterpieces!

All the beautiful fairy tales and masterpieces that you have encountered during your childhood remain as warm memories in your adulthood. This time, let's indulge in the world of masterpieces through English. You can enjoy the depth and beauty of original works, which you can't enjoy through Chinese translations.

The stories are easy for you to understand because of your familiarity with them. When you enjoy reading, your ability to understand English will also rapidly improve.

This series of *Let's Enjoy Masterpieces* is a special reading comprehension booster program, devised to improve reading comprehension for beginners whose command of English is not satisfactory, or who are elementary, middle, and high school students. With this program, you can enjoy reading masterpieces in English with fun and efficiency.

This carefully planned program is composed of 5 levels, from the beginner level of 350 words to the intermediate and advanced levels of 1,000 words. With this program's level-by-level system, you are able to read famous texts in English and to savor the true pleasure of the world's language.

The program is well conceived, composed of reader-friendly explanations of English expressions and grammar, quizzes to help the student learn vocabulary and understand the meaning of the texts, and fabulous illustrations that adorn every page. In addition, with our "Guide to Listening," not only is reading comprehension enhanced but also listening comprehension skills are highlighted.

In the audio recording of the book, texts are vividly read by professional American actors. The texts are rewritten, according to the levels of the readers by an expert editorial staff of native speakers, on the basis of standard American English with the ministry of education recommended vocabulary. Therefore, it will be of great help even for all the students that want to learn English.

Please indulge yourself in the fun of reading and listening to English through *Let's Enjoy Masterpieces*.

Introduction

托爾斯泰 Lev Nikolayevich Tolstoy
(1828~1910)

Lev Nikolayevich Tolstoy (Leo Tolstoy) is one of Russia's greatest authors and considered one of the world's greatest philosophers. Tolstoy was born into a family of aristocratic landowners. He was the fourth son of the family. After he dropped out of university, he returned home and as a landowner, he tried to improve the lives of peasants in his feudal estate.

However, after he failed to realize his ideals, he began to live promiscuously, and then in 1857, he joined the army and served in actual military campaigns.

During this period, his experiences of war influenced Tolstoy to write a lot of works that provided comprehensive insight into life and death, ethnic issues, and massacres.

When he left the army service in 1855, he was already acknowledged as a rising new talent in literature. After his marriage in 1862, he began to concentrate on writing. His major works are *War and Peace*, *Anna Karenina*, and *Resurrection*.

His writings include common themes of universal love, good and evil, religion and distrust, and the meaning of death and life. Tolstoy used his particular power of persuasion to deal with these themes in an easy-to-understand and interesting manner.

During the 82 years of his life, Tolstoy wrote around 90 works, Tolstoy, along with Dostoevsky, is regarded as one of Russia's greatest novelists.

What Men Live By and *Ivan the Fool* represent the best of Tolstoy's short works.

What Men Live By reflects Tolstoy's perspective views on religion. Through the experiences of Angle Mikhail in the human world, Tolstoy addressed the question of what people live by, and he gave his answer: People live by love.

The story of **Ivan the Fool** (1885) is written in the form of a folk tale, in which silly but honest and hard-working Ivan rises to success, exceeding his two vulgar, greedy brothers, thanks to his dedication to hard work. In this story, Tolstoy described, in a lucid and simple manner, the perfect human aspects of "Ivan the Fool."

Tolstoy's short stories are a joy to read, because they allow readers to reflect upon their lives carefully and sincerely. The stories easily and beautifully depict issues such as responsibility, love, friendship, and the sanctity of labor done by ordinary people living their daily lives.

HOW TO USE THIS BOOK
本書使用說明

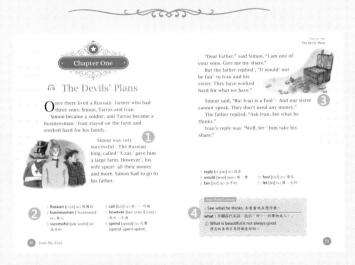

1 Original English texts

It is easy to understand the meaning of the text, because the text is rewritten according to the levels of the readers.

2 Explanation of the vocabulary

The words and expressions that include vocabulary above the elementary level are clearly defined.

3 Response notes

Spaces are included in the book so you can take notes about what you don't understand or what you want to remember.

4 One point lesson

In-depth analyses of major grammar points and expressions help you to understand sentences with difficult grammar.

🎧 *Audio Recording*

In the audio recording, native speakers narrate the texts in standard American English. By combining the written words and the audio recording, you can listen to English with great ease.

Audio books have been popular in Britain and America for many decades. They allow the listener to experience the proper word pronunciation and sentence intonation that add important meaning and drama to spoken English. Students will benefit from listening to the recording twenty or more times.

After you are familiar with the text and recording, listen once more with your eyes closed to check your listening comprehension. Finally, after you can listen with your eyes closed and understand every word and every sentence, you are then ready to mimic the native speaker.

Then you should make a recording by reading the text yourself. Then play both recordings to compare your oral skills with those of a native speaker.

HOW TO IMPROVE READING ABILITY
如何增進英文閱讀能力

1 *Catch key words*

Read the key words in the sentences and practice catching the gist of the meaning of the sentence. You might question how working with a few important words could enhance your reading ability. However, it's quite effective. If you continue to use this method, you will find out that the key words and your knowledge of people and situations enables you to understand the sentence.

2 *Divide long sentences*

Read in chunks of meaning, dividing sentences into meaningful chunks of information. In the book, chunks are arranged in sentences according to meaning. If you consider the sentences backwards or grammatically, your reading speed will be slow and you will find it difficult to listen to English.

You are ready to move to a more sophisticated level of comprehension when you find that narrowly focusing on chunks is irritating. Instead of considering the chunks, you will make it a habit to read the sentence from the beginning to the end to figure out the meaning of the whole.

③ Make inferences and assumptions

Making inferences and assumptions is part of your ability. If you don't know, try to guess the meaning of the words. Although you don't know all the words in context, don't go straight to the dictionary. Developing an ability to make inferences in the context is important.

The first way to figure out the meaning of a word is from its context. If you cannot make head or tail out of the meaning of a word, look at what comes before or after it. Ask yourself what can happen in such a situation. Make your best guess as to the word's meaning. Then check the explanations of the word in the book or look up the word in a dictionary.

④ Read a lot and reread the same book many times

There is no shortcut to mastering English. Only if you do a lot of reading will you make your way to the summit. Read fun and easy books with an average of less than one new word per page. Try to immerse yourself in English as often as you can.

Spend time "swimming" in English. Language learning research has shown that immersing yourself in English will help you improve your English, even though you may not be aware of what you're learning.

CONTENTS

Ivan the Fool

Appendixes

What Men Live By

人靠什麼活下去

Before You Read

Simon

I am a simple shoemaker who lives in the Russian countryside. Life is difficult because it is hard to make money. Martha, my wife, and I try to live as best as we can. But our life has changed a little after I met a naked young man.

Michael

I am an angel from Heaven. God tells me to gather good people's souls when they die, and bring them to Heaven. Once, I did not want to bring a mother's soul to Heaven. So God sent me to live with Simon so that I could understand God's plan for humans.

Martha

I am Simon's wife. Simon is a good man most of the time, but sometimes he makes me angry. For example, he should be stronger in his business. He lets his customers delay their payment too long!

Rich Gentleman

I am a rich noble, who can afford the finest things in Europe! If people do not do what I want, I can have them punished because I have many friends in the government.

Woman who raises two daughters

My neighbors died and left their two babies all alone. So we adopted them and raised them as our daughters. I love them very much, as if they were my own.

Chapter One

🎧 1

Simon, a Shoemaker

In old Russia, there was once an old shoemaker[1] named Simon. He and his wife were not rich.

One day in the late fall, Simon left his house to buy a winter coat. He and his wife needed a new coat to share[2].

1. **shoemaker** [`ʃuːmeɪkə(r)] (n.) 鞋匠
2. **share** [ʃer] (v.) 分享
3. **ruble** [ruːbl] (n.) 盧布（俄貨幣單位）
4. **plan to** 計畫；打算
5. **customer** [`kʌstəmə(r)] (n.) 顧客
6. **on the way** 在路上
7. **owe** [ou] (v.) 欠錢

He had only three rubles[3], but he also planned to[4] visit some of his customers[5] on the way[6]. They owed[7] him five rubles for work he had already done.

Simon went to several[8] customers' houses, but he could only collect[9] about twenty kopeks[10].

When the shoemaker went to the store to buy a coat, he did not have enough money. He asked if he could pay part of the money now and the rest later.

But the shopkeeper[11] said, "Bring all the money at once[12]. You and I both know it is difficult to collect promised[13] money."

8. **several** [`sevrəl] (a.) 幾個的
9. **collect** [kə`lekt] (v.) 收集
10. **kopek** 戈比（蘇聯的貨幣單位，為 1/100 的盧布）
11. **shopkeeper** [`ʃɑːpkiːpə(r)] (n.) 零售商店老闆
12. **at once** 同時；馬上
13. **promise** [`prɑːmɪs] (v.) 承諾

One Point Lesson

He asked if he could pay part of the money now and the rest later.
他問是否可以先支付一半的金額，剩下的下次再付。

連接詞 if（是否），用於連接間接問句，與 whether 有相同的意義。

Ask him if the rumor is true. 問問他那傳聞是不是事實。

Simon felt frustrated[1]. He spent the twenty kopeks on[2] vodka, and started walking home. Even though[3] it was getting dark now, the vodka kept[4] him warm.

As Simon was walking, he came near a small church by[5] the road. He saw something white behind the church. It looked like a man without clothes! Suddenly, Simon felt afraid.

"Robbers[6] must have killed him and taken his clothes," Simon thought. "I must hurry or they will catch me, too!"

1. **frustrated** [`frʌstreɪtɪd] (a.)
   挫敗的；洩氣的
2. **spend** A **on** B 將 A 花在 B 上
3. **even though** 即使；雖然
4. **keep** [ki:p] (v.) 使保持（狀態）
5. **by** [baɪ] (prep.) 在……旁邊
6. **robber** [`rɑ:bə(r)] (n.) 強盜

One Point Lesson

🔹 I must hurry **or** they will catch me, too!
　我得趕緊走，免得也被他們抓住！

對等連接詞 **or**（或者），若用於命令句之後，意思是「否則……」。

🔹 Study hard, **or** you'll fail in the exam.
　用功讀書，否則你考試會考不過。

Simon hurried[1] past[2] the church. After a while[3], he looked back[4].

"What should I do?" thought Simon. "If I go back there, he might kill me for my clothes. Even if he doesn't attack me, what can I do for him?"

So Simon ran down the road, out of sight[5].

At the top of the next hill[6], he suddenly stopped.

"What am I doing?" Simon thought. "The man could be dying! I should be ashamed of[7] myself!" Simon turned around and went back to the church.

---

1. **hurry** [ˋhɜːri] (v.) 趕緊；匆忙
2. **past** [pæst] (prep.) 通過；經過
3. **after a while** 過了一會
4. **look back** 回頭看
5. **out of sight** 看不見
6. **hill** [hɪl] (n.) 小丘；斜坡
7. **be ashamed of** 對……感到羞恥
8. **take off** 脫下
9. **extra** [ˋɛkstrə] (a.) 額外的
10. **a pair of boots** 一雙靴子

When Simon went behind the church, he saw a young man there. This young man was tall and healthy, but he looked afraid.

He was very handsome, with a kind face. Suddenly, Simon liked the young man. Simon took off[8] his old jacket and put it around the young man's shoulders. Simon also had an extra[9] pair of boots[10], which he gave to the young man.

"Can you walk?" asked Simon.

The man stood up and looked kindly at Simon, but he did not speak.

"Why don't you talk? Where are you from[1]?" asked Simon.

The man replied with a calm[2] and kind voice. "I'm not from around here," he said.

"I thought so," said Simon. "I know everyone in this area[3]. How did you get here[4]?"

"I cannot say," replied the man. "All I can say is that God is punishing[5] me."

1. **be from** 從……來
2. **calm** [kɑːm] (a.) 平靜的
3. **area** [`erɪə] (n.) 地區
4. **get here** 到這裡
5. **punish** [`pʌnɪʃ] (v.) 懲罰
6. **rule** [ruːl] (v.) 統治；支配
7. **at least** 至少
8. **stranger** [`streɪndʒə(r)] (n.) 陌生人
9. **worry about** 擔心……

"Of course," said Simon. "God rules[6] all men. But if you have nowhere to go, come home with me and at least[7] make yourself warm."

As Simon walked home with the stranger[8], he worried about[9] his wife.

Martha, Simon's wife, heard Simon come into the house. She smelled[10] vodka and also noticed that Simon did not have a winter coat.

"And who is this stranger he brought[11] home?" Martha thought. "Another drunk[12] he met in the bar[13]?" Martha was very disappointed[14].

10. **smell** [smel] (v.) 聞出；嗅到
11. **bring** [brɪŋ] (v.) 帶來
    (bring-brought-brought)
12. **drunk** [drʌŋk] (n.) 酒鬼
13. **bar** [bɑː(r)] (n.) 酒吧
14. **disappointed** [ˌdɪsəˋpɔɪntɪd]
    (a.) 失望的；沮喪的

"Martha," said Simon. "Let's have some supper if it is ready."

Martha became very angry. "You are late coming home, so the food is not ready. Not only are you late, but you don't have a coat. You spent all our money on vodka and you bring a strange man home. He doesn't even have clothes of his own[1]! I have no supper for drunks like you!"

"That's enough, Martha," said Simon. He tried to explain himself[2], but she was too angry.

"I should never have married you," she said. "What are we going to do this winter without a coat? And all you can do is bring drunken strangers to eat what little food we have!"

---

1. **of one's own** 屬於自己的
2. **explain oneself**
   為自己的行為辯解
3. **naked** [ˋneɪkɪd] (a.) 裸體的
4. **come from** 來自 (= be from)
5. **edge** [edʒ] (n.) 邊緣
6. **bench** [bentʃ] (n.) 長凳;長椅
7. **lap** [læp] (n.)
   坐時自腰至膝蓋部分
8. **look down** 俯視
9. **floor** [flɔ:(r)] (n.) 地板;地面
10. **pitiful** [ˋpɪtɪfl] (a.) 令人同情的

Then Martha looked at the stranger. She said, "If he were a good man, he would not be naked[3]. And you would tell me where he came from[4]!"

"That's what I'm trying to tell you!" said Simon. He then told his wife how he met the young man.

As Martha listened to her husband, she looked at the young man. He sat on the edge[5] of the bench[6] without moving. His hands were in his lap[7], and he looked down[8] at the floor[9]. He looked very pitiful[10].

After Simon told his story, he said, "Martha, don't you love God?"

When Martha heard these words, she had compassion[1] for the stranger. She went back into[2] the kitchen and got some tea and bread. She put them in front of the stranger.

"Eat, if you want to," she said. As Martha looked at the young man eating, she did not feel angry anymore. She thought she could like this young man.

Suddenly, the stranger looked up[3] and smiled. A light[4] seemed to come from his face. "Thank you," he said.

---

1. **compassion** [kəm`pæʃən] (n.)
   憐憫；同情
2. **go back into** 回到……裡
3. **look up** 往上看

4. **light** [laɪt] (n.) 光線；光亮
5. **stay** [steɪ] (v.) 留下；暫住
6. **skill** [skɪl] (n.) 技術；技能

The stranger stayed[5] and learned how to make shoes from Simon. He learned quickly and had great skill[6]. He only told them that his name was Michael.

Michael made shoes so well that many people came to Simon's shop. Soon Simon and Martha had enough money for food and clothes.

A True or False.

T F **1** Simon and his wife had a lot of money.

T F **2** The naked young man looked very angry.

T F **3** Martha was very angry when she saw her husband bring a stranger home.

T F **4** The young man, Michael, learned how to make shoes from Simon.

T F **5** Michael became a fine shoemaker.

B Fill in the blanks with the given words.

spend   look   owe   leave

1 One day in the late fall, Simon _____ his house to buy a coat.

2 They _____ him five rubles for work he had done.

3 He _____ the twenty kopeks on vodka, and started walking home.

4 The young man was tall and heathy, but _____ afraid.

C Match the two parts of each sentence.

1 Michael was cold • • a because he was naked.

2 When Martha smelled vodka, she thought • • b after he felt ashamed.

3 Simon went back to the church • • c so he smiled at her.

4 Martha gave the stranger food • • d that Simon had spent all their money in a bar.

D Choose the correct answer.

1 Why didn't Simon help Michael when he first saw him?

(a) Simon thought Michael was a robber.

(b) Simon wanted to get home fast because he was cold.

(c) Simon was afraid of being robbed.

2 Which is NOT one of the reasons Martha was angry with Simon when he came home?

(a) She knew Simon had been drinking vodka because she could smell it.

(b) Simon came home very late.

(c) She thought Simon had a secret lover.

Heavenly Creatures—
The Angels

Michael, the angel who visits Simon and his wife in this story, is the strongest of all the angels. Long before God created mankind, He created angels.

These creatures look like humans, but they have large white wings. They are usually clothed in white, shining robes. In fact, humans cannot look directly at an angel's face, because a bright light seems to come from their heads and bodies.

Angels are the servants of God. Their main job is to tell God's message to human beings.

Angels tell people about God's love and try to help them. Their other job is to lead dead souls to heaven. If the person was good, the angel will visit them when they die and take their soul up to Heaven.

Sometimes, angels protect humans. They may save humans from serious accidents. That's why some people in dangerous situations pray to their 'guardian angel' for help.

Chapter Two

Angel of the Earth

After one year, a rich gentleman came to Simon's shop. He asked, "Who is the master[1] shoemaker here?"

"I am, sir," said Simon. "How can I help you?"

The rich gentleman showed Simon a large piece of very fine[2] leather.

"Do you know what kind of leather[3] this is?"

"It's good leather, sir," said Simon.

The gentleman laughed. "It is the best, you fool. I want you to make me a pair of boots that will last[4] for one year. Can you do it?"

Simon was afraid. He looked at Michael and asked, "Should we take this work?"

Michael nodded[5] his head. He seemed to be looking behind the rich gentleman, but no one was there. Suddenly, Michael smiled again.

"What are you smiling at, you fool?" shouted the rich man. "You had better[6] start working. I will come back[7] in two days!"

1. **master** [ˋmæstə(r)] (a.) 大師級的
2. **fine** [faɪn] (a.) 上好的
3. **leather** [ˋlɛðə(r)] (n.) 皮革
4. **last** [læst] (v.) 維持；夠用
5. **nod** [nɑːd] (v.) 點頭
6. **had better** 最好
7. **come back** 回來

One Point Lesson

● Do you know **what kind of leather this is?**
你知道這是什麼類的皮革嗎？

間接問句：間接問句的句型為「疑問句 + 主詞 + 動詞」，為整句中的受詞。

e.g. I asked him **how he solved the problem.**
我問他是如何解決那個問題的。

8

Michael worked on[1] the gentleman's boots the next day. When Simon checked[2] his work, he shouted in surprise[3].

"What have you done?" yelled[4] Simon. "These are slippers, not boots!"

Suddenly, there was a knock[5] at the door. Simon opened it and saw the rich man's servant.

"The gentleman's wife has sent[6] me about the boots," said the servant[7]. Simon was afraid.

"My master does not need them," continued the servant. "He is dead. My lady wants you to make slippers for his funeral."

Simon was amazed. Silently, Michael picked up the slippers he had made and gave them to the servant. The servant bowed[8], and said, "Thank you, master shoemaker."

1. **work on** 進行……工作
2. **check** [tʃek] (v.) 檢查
3. **in surprise** 驚訝地
4. **yell** [jel] (v.) 叫喊；吼叫
5. **knock** [nɑːk] (n.) 敲；擊打
6. **send** [send] (v.) 派遣
7. **servant** [ˋsɜːrvənt] (n.) 僕人
8. **bow** [baʊ] (v.) 鞠躬；欠身

9

Michael had now lived with Simon for six years. One day, he stood looking out the window. Simon was curious[1]. Michael had never before been interested in the outside[2] world.

"Look," said Martha, "Here comes a woman with two daughters. One of the daughters has a bad leg."

The woman came into the shoemaker's shop. "Good day to you," said Simon. "What can we do for you?"

"I want leather shoes for these girls," said the woman.

"We can do that," said Simon. He noticed[3] that Michael was looking at the girls very closely[4].

1. curious [`kjʊriəs] (a.) 好奇的
2. outside [ˌaʊt`saɪd] (a.) 外面的
3. notice [`noʊtɪs] (v.) 注意到
4. closely [kloʊsli] (adv.) 接近地
5. hurt [hɜːrt] (v.) 使受傷
6. be born 天生的
7. twin [twɪn] (n.) 雙胞胎之一
8. give birth to 生孩子
9. roll [roʊl] (v.) 滾動
10. on top of 在……之上
11. twist [twɪst] (v.) 扭傷
12. since [sɪns] (conj.) 自……以來
13. unfortunately[ʌn`fɔːrtʃənətli] (adv.) 不幸地
14. raise [reɪz] (v.) 養育

"How did this girl hurt[5] her leg?" asked Simon. "Was she born[6] that way?"

"No," said the woman. "Her mother did that. I am not their real mother. These girls are the children of our neighbors. They are twins[7], born just about six years ago. Their father died one week before they were born. And their mother died right after she gave birth to[8] them. As she died, she rolled[9] on top of[10] one of the girls and twisted[11] the baby's leg.

Since[12] I just had a baby of my own, I was able to feed them. Unfortunately[13], my baby died, but I raised[14] these two girls. Now I love them like they were my own."

10

Martha said, "It is true that one may live without a father or mother, but one cannot live without God."

Suddenly, a bright light filled[1] the room. Everyone looked at Michael, who was the source[2] of this light. He was smiling and looking up at the heavens[3].

Michael put down[4] his tools[5] and took off his apron[6]. He bowed to Simon and Martha.

"God has forgiven[7] me," he said. "I am sorry to leave you, but I must go now."

1. **fill** [fɪl] (v.) 充滿
2. **source** [sɔːrs] (n.) 來源
3. **heaven** [ˋhɛvn] (n.) 天空；天堂
4. **put down** 放下
5. **tool** [tuːl] (n.) 用具
6. **apron** [ˋeɪprən] (n.) 工作圍裙
7. **forgive** [fərˋgɪv] (v.) 原諒 (forgive-forgave-forgiven)
8. **keep** [kiːp] (v.) 留住

Simon said to Michael, "I can see now that you are not a common man, and I cannot keep[8] you. But please, tell me your story, if you can."

Michael smiled at Simon.

"I owe you an explanation[9] at least. You see, six years ago, God punished me because I disobeyed[10] him. He sent me to take the soul[11] of a woman. This woman was the mother of the twins who were just here.

When I came to her house, I saw the two newborn[12] babies. The mother begged[13] me not to take her soul. So I flew back to Heaven and asked God to save[14] her."

9. **explanation** [ɛkspləˈneɪʃən] (n.) 說明；解釋
10. **disobey** [ˌdɪsəˈbeɪ] (v.) 違反
11. **soul** [soʊl] (n.) 靈魂；心靈

12. **newborn** [ˈnuːbɔːrn] (a.) 新生的
13. **beg** [bɛg] (v.) 懇求
14. **save** [seɪv] (v.) 救；挽救

One Point Lesson

The mother begged me **not to take** her soul.
那母親哀求我不要帶走她的靈魂。

「**to**（不定詞）＋動詞原形」的否定：否定語（not、never）須放在不定詞的前面。

e.g. I promised **never to tell** a lie again.
我答應再也不說謊了。

"God told me, 'Go back and take the mother's soul. Then you must learn three truths[1]. First, learn what lives in man. Second, learn what is not given to man. Finally, learn what men live by[2]. When you have learned these things, you may return to heaven.'

So I flew back to the woman's cottage[3]. I took her soul, and then I suddenly lost my wings! I fell to the earth. That is how you found me, Simon, naked and freezing[4] behind the church.

I was very lonely and afraid. I thought that you could not help me. But you came back and gave me your clothes!

Then when I came home with you, I was afraid of Martha. She seemed very angry. But she pitied[5] me and offered[6] what little food you had. Then I smiled because I had learned the first of God's truths. Love lives in men."

1. **truth** [tru:θ] (n.) 真理
2. **what men live by**
   人賴以為生的東西
3. **cottage** [ˋkɑːtɪdʒ] (n.)
   小屋；農舍

4. **freezing** [ˋfriːzɪŋ] (a.) 極冷的
5. **pity** [ˋpɪti] (v.) 憐憫；同情
6. **offer** [ˋɔːfə(r)] (v.) 給予；提供

Then after a year, the rich gentleman visited us. I saw the angel of death behind him. The man was about to[1] die, yet he wanted boots that would last for a year. Then I realized[2] that men are not given the knowledge[3] to know what they need. I smiled then, because I had learned the second truth.

Just now, I learned the third truth when that woman arrived. She loved these children, even though they were not hers. I could see that God lived in her. Then I understood that men live by love. So I smiled for the third time."

Michael seemed to grow[4] taller. A bright light shone from his whole body. Simon and Martha could not look directly[5] at him. Wings grew from his body. Michael's voice grew stronger and loud.

1. **be about to** 即將
2. **realize** [ˋrɪəlaɪz] (v.) 領悟
3. **knowledge** [ˋnɑːlɪdʒ] (n.) 理解
4. **grow** [ɡroʊn] (v.) 生長
5. **directly** [dəˋrɛktli] (adv.) 直接地
6. **roof** [ruːf] (n.) 屋頂
7. **a ray of light** 一道光線
8. **spread** [sprɛd] (v.) 展開；張開 (spread-spread-spread)

"I now understand that men live by love alone. He who has love is with God, and God is in him, for God is love."

Then the roof[6] of the shop opened and a ray of light[7] fell down from heaven. Michael spread[8] his wings and flew up into the light.

Simon and Martha covered their eyes and fell to the ground. When Simon opened his eyes again, the roof was closed. There was no one in the shop but he and his wife.

A Match.

1 ashamed •

2 calm •

3 kind •

4 frustrated •

5 afraid •

6 pity •

• a relaxed

• b gentle

• c disappointed

• d embarrassed

• e sympathy

• f scared

B Fill in the blanks with the given words.

out of   inside   behind   outside   from

1 The angel of death was _____ the rich gentleman.

2 Michael stood before the window looking _____.

3 The woman with the twins came _____ the shop.

4 Wings grew _____ Michael's shoulders.

5 A light came down _____ heaven.

C Rearrange the following truths in the order that Michael learned.

❶ Love lives in men.

❷ Men live by love.

❸ Men are not given the knowledge of what they need.

_____ ⇨ _____ ⇨ _____

D Choose the correct answer.

❶ How did Michael learn the final truth?

(a) He met a rich gentleman who ordered an expensive pair of boots.

(b) He heard a story about a woman who loved her adopted children.

(c) Simon told him a story about love.

❷ What was NOT something that happened each time Michael learned a truth?

(a) His face became brighter.

(b) He smiled.

(c) His wings grew a little longer.

Ivan the Fool

傻子伊凡

Before You Read

Ivan

My name is Ivan, and I am a farmer in Russia. People say I'm a fool, but I don't care. I just work hard every day to make enough food for my family.

Simon

My name is Simon, and I was the greatest soldier in all of Russia! My armies won many battles! But the Devil tricked me when I fought against India.

Tarras

I am Tarras, Russia's wealthiest merchant! Well, at least I was rich until the Devil competed against me in business. But now I live in Ivan's house.

The Devil

I am the Devil, and I enjoy making people greedy for gold and other worldly pleasures! But I could not make Ivan want anything! Ivan is too simple for me! He makes me crazy!

The little Devils

We are the devil brothers and we do everything the Devil tells us. We have fun ruining people's lives! Simon and Tarras were no match for us! But Ivan is too stubborn and simple! He caught each one of us and made us give him something. When the Devil finds us, he will punish us!

· Chapter One ·

🎧13 The Devils' Plans

Once there lived a Russian[1] farmer who had three sons: Simon, Tarras and Ivan.

Simon became a soldier, and Tarras became a businessman[2]. Ivan stayed on the farm and worked hard for his family.

Simon was very successful[3]. The Russian king, called[4] 'Czar,' gave him a large farm. However[5], his wife spent[6] all their money and more. Simon had to go to his father.

---

1. **Russian** [rʌʃən] (a.) 俄國的
2. **businessman** [ˋbɪznəsmən] (n.) 商人
3. **successful** [səkˋsesfəl] (a.) 成功的
4. **call** [kɔːl] (v.) 把……叫做
5. **however** [hauˋevə(r)] (conj.) 然而；不過
6. **spend** [spend] (v.) 花費 (spend-spent-spent)

"Dear Father," said Simon, "I am one of your sons. Give me my share."

But the father replied[7], "It would[8] not be fair[9] to Ivan and his sister. They have worked hard for what we have."

Simon said, "But Ivan is a fool[10]. And our sister cannot speak. They don't need any money."

The father replied, "Ask Ivan. See what he thinks."

Ivan's reply was: "Well, let[11] him take his share."

7. **reply** [rɪ`plaɪ] (v.) 回答
8. **would** [wʊd] (aux.) 將；會
9. **fair** [fer] (a.) 公平的
10. **fool** [fuːl] (n.) 傻瓜
11. **let** [let] (v.) 讓；允許

One Point Lesson

◆ See what he thinks. 去看看他在想什麼。

what：作關係代名詞，表示「所……的事物或人。」

e.g. **What is beautiful** is not always good.
漂亮的東西不見得都是好的。

Soon, the other brother, Tarras, came home. He said to his father, "Simon took his share. What about[1] me?"

Again, the father refused[2], saying, "You, like[3] Simon, have not worked on our farm."

Tarras then spoke to Ivan. "Give me half[4] of your grain[5] and only one horse."

Ivan said, "Fine. Take what is your fair share." Tarras took what he asked for[6] and left[7].

1. **what about . . . ?**
   那……如何呢？
2. **refuse** [rɪ`fjuːz] (v.)
   拒絕；不准
3. **like** [laɪk] (prep.) 像；如
4. **half** [hæf] (n.) 一半
5. **grain** [greɪn] (n.) 穀物
6. **ask for** 要求
7. **leave** [liːv] (v.) 離開
   (leave-left-left)

8. **devil** [`dɛvl] (n.) 魔鬼；撒旦
9. **disappointed** [ˌdɪsə`pɔɪntɪd]
   (a.) 失望的
10. **argue** [`ɑːrgjuː] (v.) 爭吵
11. **each other** 彼此
12. **master** [`mæstə(r)] (n.) 主人
13. **fail in** 失敗
14. **go back to** 回去

Ivan the Fool

The Devil[8] was disappointed[9] to hear about Ivan and his brothers. He wanted people to argue[10].

So the Devil called three young devils to him. "I want you to make Ivan and his brothers fight with each other[11]," said the Devil. "Can you make them do this?"

"Yes, master[12]," they said. "We will make each brother fail in[13] his work. Then they will all go back to[14] their father's farm and argue."

One Point Lesson

> I want you to make Ivan and his brothers fight with each other.
> 我要你們去讓伊凡兄弟們吵起來。

---

make + 受詞 + 動詞原形：使變成……
make 為使役動詞，使另一個動作發生，後接受詞及動詞原形。

e.g She makes me feel happy. 她讓我感到快樂。

15

The little devils agreed that they would each ruin[1] one brother. Whoever[2] finished first would then help the others.

One month later, the first gave his report[3].

"I have succeeded[4] in my mission[5]," said the devil proudly[6]. "Tomorrow, Simon returns to his father. The first thing I did was to blow[7] some courage[8] into Simon's heart. Simon then went to the Czar and told him he would conquer[9] India. The Czar made him Chief General[10] and sent him to war.

Then, I flew to the ruler[11] of India. I showed him how to[12] make many soldiers from straw[13]. These soldiers killed many Russians.

The Czar was very angry. He put Simon in prison[14] and planned to execute[15] him tomorrow. I will help him escape[16] tonight. Now, my brothers, which one of you needs my help?"

1. **ruin** [`ruːɪn] (v.) 毀滅
2. **whoever** [huːˋevə(r)] (pron.) 無論誰
3. **report** [rɪˋpɔːrt] (n.) 報告
4. **succeed in** 成功；辦妥
5. **mission** [ˋmɪʃən] (n.) 任務
6. **proudly** [ˋpraʊdli] (adv.) 得意洋洋地
7. **blow** [bloʊ] (v.) 煽動
8. **courage** [ˋkɜːrɪdʒ] (n.) 膽量
9. **conquer** [ˋkɑːŋkə(r)] (v.) 攻克
10. **general** [ˋdʒenrəl] (n.) 將軍
11. **ruler** [ˋruːlə(r)] (n.) 統治者
12. **how to** 如何
13. **straw** [strɔː] (n.) 稻草
14. **prison** [ˋprɪzən] (n.) 監獄
15. **execute** [ˋeksɪkjuːt] (v.) 處死
16. **escape** [ɪˋskeɪp] (v.) 逃跑

"Not me," said the second devil. "My work with Tarras will be finished next week. I made him greedier[1]. He bought everything and spent all his money! Soon he will lose everything and return to his father."

The third devil looked embarrassed[2]. "My work is not going so well," he said. "I spat[3] in Ivan's morning tea to give him a terrible stomachache[4]. Still[5] he got up to plant[6] seeds[7] in his field.

1. **greedier**
   更貪婪的（greedy 的比較級）
2. **embarrassed** [ɪmˋbærəst] (a.)
   困窘的
3. **spit** [spɪt] (v.) 吐口水
   (spit-spat-spat)
4. **stomachache** [ˋstʌməkeɪk]
   (n.) 胃痛
5. **still** [stɪl] (adv.) 仍舊地

6. **plant** [plænt] (v.) 栽種
7. **seed** [siːd] (n.) 種子
8. **plow** [plaʊ] (v.) 犁；耕
9. **give up** 放棄
10. **grab** [græb] (v.) 抓住
11. **blade** [bleɪd] (n.) 刀；刀口
12. **sigh** [saɪ] (v.) 嘆息
13. **stop . . . from** 阻止；阻擋

Then I made the ground very hard. This made it very difficult for Ivan to plow[8] the field. I thought he would give up[9], but he continued.

So I went into the earth and grabbed[10] the blade[11] of the plow with my hands. But he pushed very hard, so my fingers were cut!"

The third devil sighed[12]. "Come, my brothers, and help me when you are finished. We must stop Ivan from[13] making enough food for his family."

One Point Lesson

▸ This made **it** very difficult for Ivan to plow the field.
這讓伊凡犁田犁得很辛苦。

───────────────

虛受詞 it：當句中受詞太長，就使用虛受詞 it，真正的受詞放在 it 之後。

e.g. I found **it** difficult to work all day long.
我發現要整天工作是很困難的事。

The next day, Ivan returned to his field to finish the plowing. He still had a terrible stomachache. But Ivan was a strong man, and he was used to working[1] every day.

Ivan tried to pick up[2] his plow that he left[3] in the ground last night. It would not move. In fact[4], the third devil was in the ground holding[5] it. The devil's legs were wrapped around the plow.

Ivan put his hand in the ground. He felt something soft. With his great strength[6], he pulled it out[7]. It seemed to be an ugly animal.

1. **be used to + V-ing** 習慣於
2. **pick up** 拾起
3. **leave** [liːv] (v.) 遺留下
4. **in fact** 實際上
5. **hold** [hoʊld] (v.) 抓住
6. **with one's strength** 用某人的力氣
7. **pull out** 拔出
8. **disgusted** [dɪsˋɡʌstɪd] (a.) 厭惡的；厭煩的
9. **whatever** [wɑːtˋevə(r)] (pron.) 無論……東西
10. **lower** [ˋloʊə(r)] (v.) 放下
11. **scratch** [skrætʃ] (v.) 抓；搔
12. **pain** [peɪn] (n.) 疼痛
13. **cure** [kjʊr] (v.) 治癒
14. **release** [rɪˋliːs] (v.) 釋放
15. **medicine** [ˋmedɪsən] (n.) 藥

Ivan was disgusted[8]. He raised his hand to hit the devil against the blade of the plow.

"Do not kill me!" cried the devil. "I will give you whatever[9] you want!"

Ivan lowered[10] his arm and scratched[11] his head. He said, "There is a terrible pain[12] in my stomach. Can you cure[13] it?"

"Of course!" said the devil. "Release[14] me, and I will find some medicine[15] for you."

The little creature[1] looked around and picked up some roots. He gave these to Ivan and said, "Eat these. They will cure any illness you may have."

Ivan ate some of the root. The pain in his stomach went away[2]. "Very well," said Ivan. "You may go, and God bless you[3]."

Devils hate[4] hearing God's name. The devil immediately[5] disappeared[6]. All that remained[7] was a small hole in the ground.

That evening, Ivan saw his brother Simon and his wife sitting at the dinner table.

Simon said, "Hello, Ivan. I have lost everything and have returned home. Will you care for us until I can find some work?"
"Very well," said Ivan. "You can stay with us."

As Ivan sat down, Simon's wife said to her husband, "I cannot eat with a dirty farmer who smells[8] bad."

Simon said to Ivan, "My wife cannot stand[9] your smell. You may eat on the porch[10]."
"Very well," said Ivan.

1. **creature** [`kri:tʃə(r)] (n.)
   生物；動物
2. **go away** 停止；離開
3. **God bless you.**
   上帝保佑你。
4. **hate** [heɪt] (v.) 憎恨；嫌惡
5. **immediately** [ɪ`mi:diətli]
   (adv.) 立即地
6. **disappear** [ˌdɪsə`pɪr] (v.) 消失
7. **remain** [rɪ`meɪn] (v.) 留下
8. **smell** [smel] (v.)
   發出……氣味；聞起來
9. **stand** [stænd] (v.) 忍受
10. **porch** [pɔːrtʃ] (n.) 門廊；陽台

A Choose the words in the list that related to Simon, Ivan, and Tarras.

a stomachache **b** soldier **c** courage **d** generous
e farmer **f** greedy **g** defeat **h** businessman

Simon   Ivan   Tarras

❶_____   ❷_____   ❸_____

B True or False.

T F ❶ Ivan is simple, but tough and hard-working.

T F ❷ The devil made Tarras greedier.

T F ❸ Ivan's father wants to divide his farm between his three sons.

T F ❹ Simon defeated India.

C Choose the correct answer.

❶ Why did Simon want a share of his father's farm?

(a) He was very greedy.

(b) His wife spent all his money.

(c) He needed money to raise an army.

❷ What things did Tarras take for his share of the farm?

(a) Half of Ivan's.

(b) Half the cows and half the horses.

(c) One horse and half the grain.

D Rewrite the sentences in past perfect tense.

> Ivan *left* his plow standing in the ground.
> ⇨ clvan *had left* his plow standing in the ground.

❶ Simon didn't work on the farm.

⇨ _____

❷ The Devil was disappointed to hear about Ivan.

⇨ _____

❸ The pain in his stomach went away.

⇨ _____

Another Angels—

The Devils

The Devil tried to ruin Ivan's life by making him and his people greedy for gold. In Christian mythology, this behavior is typical for the Devil.

The most common story about the Devil says that a long time ago, he was God's strongest angel. His original name was Lucifer.

Lucifer decided that he was stronger and better than God. He convinced many other angels to join him in his fight against God. However, God and his loyal angels were stronger, and Lucifer lost the battle.

God threw Lucifer and the disloyal angels out of Heaven. They fell down to Hell. This is why Lucifer and the angels who followed him are called 'fallen angels.' When they were thrown out of Heaven, God changed their appearance. They became like beasts.

Devils are usually pictured with a pitchfork. Devils use their pitchforks to gather human souls after people have died. So if you lead a bad life, you might see the Devil when you die!

Chapter Two

🎧 19 Ivan vs. the Devils

After finishing his mission, the first devil went to Ivan's farm. However, he could not find his brother.

"Something must have happened[1] to my brother. I will have to stop Ivan myself," said the first devil, seeing the small hole in the ground.

The little devil flooded[2] the meadow[3] with water. Ivan tried to cut the grass, but it was very difficult. Soon he became tired.

He said to himself, "I will come back here and will not leave until I have cut all the grass."

The small devil hid[4] in the grass and Ivan soon returned. As Ivan swung[5] a sickle[6] down, the devil buried[7] the tip of the blade in the earth. With great effort[8], Ivan pulled the blade free. The devil jumped out of the way, but Ivan cut off [9] part of his tail.

1. **happen** [ˋhæpən] (v.)
   發生
2. **flood** [flʌd] (v.) 淹沒；氾濫
3. **meadow** [ˋmedoʊ] (n.)
   （牧）草地
4. **hide** [haɪd] (v.) 躲藏
   (hide-hid-hidden)
5. **swing** [swɪŋ] (v.) 揮舞；揮
   (swing-swung-swung)
6. **sickle** [ˋsɪkl] (n.) 鐮刀
7. **bury** [ˋberi] (v.) 埋藏
8. **with effort** 用盡力氣
9. **cut off** 切斷；切除

One Point Lesson

◆ Something **must have happened** to my brother.
我兄弟一定是發生了什麼事。

must have + p.p.：一定是……；必定發生過……：強烈確信某件事情已經發生。

e.g She **must have come** back home. 她一定已經回到家了。

20

For the rest[1] of the day, the devil tried to stop Ivan. But Ivan finally finished his work.

"Now I will start to plant the oats[2]," said Ivan.

The devil thought, "I will certainly[3] stop him tomorrow!"

When the devil woke up, he saw that Ivan had planted the oats during the night!

"He does not even sleep!" the devil said to himself.

"I must think ahead[4]. Ivan will soon need hay[5]. So I will make his hay rotten[6] before he comes to the barn[7]."

After wetting the hay to make it go bad[8], the devil fell asleep[9].

The next day, Ivan came to the barn with a long pitchfork[10] to pick up the hay. He stuck[11] the pitchfork into the hay and felt it hit something solid[12]. At the same time[13], there was a strange cry.

1. **the rest** 剩餘部分
2. **oat** [out] (n.) 燕麥
3. **certainly** [ˋsɜːrtnli] (adv.) 無疑地
4. **ahead** [ˋəhed] (adv.) 在前地
5. **hay** [heɪ] (n.) 乾草
6. **rotten** [ˋrɑːtn] (a.) 腐爛的
7. **barn** [bɑːrn] (n.) 糧倉；穀倉
8. **go bad** 開始腐壞
9. **fall asleep** 沈睡
10. **pitchfork** [ˋpɪtʃfɔːrk] (n.) 乾草叉
11. **stick** [stɪk] (v.) 刺；戳 (stick-stuck-stuck)
12. **solid** [ˋsɑːlɪd] (a.) 固體的；堅固的
13. **at the same time** 同時

There was a little devil stuck in the fork! Ivan shouted, "You said you would go away!"

"I am another one," said the devil. "You met my brother before."

21

"I do not care[1] who you are. I will kill you anyway," said Ivan.

"Please don't!" cried the devil.

"I can make you soldiers from straw!"

"What are soldiers good for[2]?" asked Ivan.

"They can do almost[3] anything for you," replied the devil.

"Then show me how to make them," Ivan said.

The little devil rubbed[4] straw together and said some magic words[5]. Soon there were many soldiers marching around the barn.

"Now let me go," said the devil.

"Wait," said Ivan. "Many soldiers need a lot of food. How do I turn them back to[6] straw?"

"Just say the words: 'So many soldiers, so much straw.' Then they will disappear," said the devil.

"Fine," said Ivan. "You may[7] go, and God bless you." As soon as Ivan said 'God', the little devil disappeared into the ground. All that was left was a small hole.

1. **care** [ker] (v.) 關心；在乎
2. **be good for** 有益於
3. **almost** [`ɔ:lmoust] (adv.) 幾乎；差不多
4. **rub** [rʌb] (v.) 摩擦；揉
5. **magic word** 咒語
6. **turn** A **back to** B 把 A 變回 B
7. **may** [meɪ] (aux.) 可以

One Point Lesson

◆ **As soon as** Ivan said 'God', the little devil disappeared into the ground.
當伊凡一說到「上帝」，小惡魔就遁地消失了。

as soon as：一⋯⋯就⋯⋯

e.g. I'll ask him **as soon as** he comes back.
等他一回到家，我就會問他。

Ivan the Fool

22

Ivan returned home and was surprised to see his brother Tarras and his wife. Tarras seemed embarrassed because he had lost all his money.

"Hello, Ivan," he said. "May we stay here until I can start a new business?"

Ivan agreed. "Yes, you are welcome to[1] stay here as long as[2] you want."

Then Ivan sat down to eat. But Tarras's wife made a bad face[3] . "I cannot eat with such a smelly[4] farmer," she said.

Tarras said, "Ivan, my wife cannot eat with you. Go to the porch and eat by yourself[5] ."

"Alright," said Ivan. "I have to feed[6] the horses soon anyway."

1. **be welcome to** 可隨意地做
2. **as long as** 只要
3. **make a face** 做鬼臉
4. **smelly** [ˋsmeli] (a.) 臭的
5. **by oneself** 單獨地
6. **feed** [fiːd] (v.) 餵

73

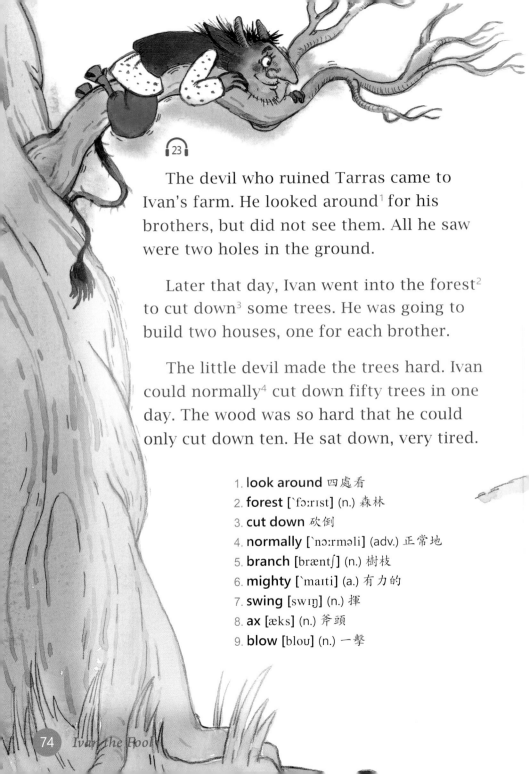

🎧 23

The devil who ruined Tarras came to Ivan's farm. He looked around[1] for his brothers, but did not see them. All he saw were two holes in the ground.

Later that day, Ivan went into the forest[2] to cut down[3] some trees. He was going to build two houses, one for each brother.

The little devil made the trees hard. Ivan could normally[4] cut down fifty trees in one day. The wood was so hard that he could only cut down ten. He sat down, very tired.

1. **look around** 四處看
2. **forest** [`fɔːrɪst] (n.) 森林
3. **cut down** 砍倒
4. **normally** [`nɔːrməli] (adv.) 正常地
5. **branch** [bræntʃ] (n.) 樹枝
6. **mighty** [`maɪti] (a.) 有力的
7. **swing** [swɪŋ] (n.) 揮
8. **ax** [æks] (n.) 斧頭
9. **blow** [bloʊ] (n.) 一擊

The little devil was watching Ivan from high up in a tree.

"Ivan is too tired to continue. If the brothers have to live in one house, they will argue."

The little devil began to dance for joy in the branches[5]. He did not see Ivan stand up. With a mighty[6] swing[7] of his ax[8], Ivan hit the tree.

Before the devil could escape, the tree was cut in one blow[9]. The little devil fell down and Ivan found it.

◦ The wood was **so** hard **that** he **could** only cut down ten.
樹木實在太硬了，所以他只砍了十棵。

so . . . that . . . can (cannot) :
實在太……，所以只能（無法）……。

e.g. I was **so** busy **that I couldn't** get in touch with you.
我實在太忙了，所以無法和你聯絡。

24

"What's this?" Ivan cried. "I thought you went away!"

"I am another one!"

"Well," said Ivan. "It doesn't matter[1]. I will kill you with my ax."

"Please, do not kill me," cried the devil. "I can create[2] gold for you."

"Show me how," said Ivan.

The devil told Ivan to gather leaves from a special oak tree[3]. He showed Ivan how to rub the leaves in his hands. When the devil said some magic words, the leaves changed to gold coins[4]!

"This is a great trick[5]," said Ivan. "The village children will really like this."

"Now please let me go," begged the devil.

"With God's blessing[6], you may go," said Ivan.

At the mention[7] of the name of God, the devil disappeared into the earth[8].

1. **It doesn't matter.**
   沒差／無所謂。
2. **create** [kri`eɪt] (v.) 製造
3. **oak tree** 橡樹
4. **gold coin** 金幣
5. **trick** [trɪk] (n.) 把戲

6. **blessing** [`blesɪŋ] (n.)
   （神的）恩賜；祝福
7. **mention** [`menʃən] (n.)
   提及；說到
8. **earth** [ɜːrθ] (n.) 土；泥

25

Ivan soon finished building the houses for his brothers to move into. When he completed[1] his field work, he planned a big feast[2]. He asked his brothers to come to a party, but they refused. Ivan had a party anyway, and invited all the villagers[3]. He decided to[4] entertain[5] them.

Ivan told the village girls to sing songs for him. He said he would pay them well. The girls sang and then asked him for some reward[6].

"I'll show you soon." Ivan went into the forest while the girls laughed at[7] him. Soon Ivan came back with a large bag. He pulled out many gold coins from the bag and threw them into the air[8].

The villagers were very surprised. Then they started fighting for the coins on the ground. Now it was Ivan's turn to laugh at them.

Still laughing, he told the children he would make some soldiers sing for them. He went into the barn and came out with many soldiers. These soldiers sang songs in beautiful voices. All the people were amazed[9].

1. **complete** [kəm`pli:t] (v.)
   完成；結束

2. **feast** [fi:st] (n.) 盛宴

3. **villager** [`vɪlɪdʒə(r)] (n.) 村民

4. **decide to** 決定做

5. **entertain** [ˌentər`teɪn] (v.)
   娛樂；款待

6. **reward** [rɪ`wɔ:rd] (n.)
   報償；獎賞

7. **laugh at** 嘲笑

8. **air** [er] (n.) 空中

9. **amazed** [ə`meɪzd] (a.)
   驚奇的；吃驚的

One Point Lesson

● **Still laughing,** he told the children he would make some soldiers sing for them.
他繼續笑著，對孩子們說要叫士兵們為他們唱歌。

分詞子句：省略與主句相同的主詞，子句中的動詞改成動名詞，形成分詞子句。這裡意指「邊做……邊……」。

e.g. **Singing and dancing together,** we had a lot of fun.
我們又唱歌又跳舞，歡度了時光。

A Match.

1 plow •
2 axe •
3 pitchfork •
4 sickle •

• a cut trees
• b pick up hay
• c break and turn over earth
• d cut grass

B Match.

1 the first devil •

2 the second devil •

3 the third devil •

• a Flooded Ivan's meadow Showed Ivan how to make soldiers

• b Gave Ivan a stomachache Gave Ivan some medicine roots

• c Made the hay rotten Showed Ivan how to make gold coins

C Fill in the blanks with the given words.

when	but	before	if	after

❶ _____ finishing his mission, the first devil went to Ivan's farm to help his brother.

❷ Ivan tried to cut the grass, _____ it was very difficult.

❸ _____ the devil woke up, he saw that Ivan had planted the oats during the night!

❹ _____ the brothers have to live in one house, they will argue.

❺ _____ the devil could escape, he was caught in the branches.

D Rearrange the following sentences in chronological order.

❶ Tarras and his wife came to Ivan's house to stay.
❷ The second devil danced for joy in the branches.
❸ The first devil flooded the meadow with water.
❹ Ivan invited all the villagers to a party.
❺ Ivan built the houses for his brothers.

_____ ⇨ _____ ⇨ _____ ⇨ _____ ⇨ _____

Chapter Three

🎧26 # Ivan, the Leader

The next morning, Simon was knocking[1] on Ivan's door.

"Brother, tell me where the soldiers came from," Simon asked.

"I will show[2] you," said Ivan. He took[3] Simon into the barn and made some soldiers from straw.

"This is amazing[4]!" said Simon. "With soldiers like these, I can defeat[5] any kingdom[6]!"

Ivan was greatly surprised. "You should have asked me before. But you must promise to take them away from[7] here. We do not have enough food to feed them."

Simon promised, and Ivan made him a huge[8] army. Finally, Simon cried, "Enough, enough. Thank you, Ivan!"

Ivan replied, "It was no trouble[9]. If you want more, just come back." Then Simon left with his army to attack[10] nearby[11] kingdoms.

1. **knock on** 敲；擊
2. **show** [ʃou] (v.) 展示；告知
3. **take** [teɪk] (v.) 引導
4. **amazing** [əˋmeɪzɪŋ] (a.) 令人吃驚的
5. **defeat** [dɪˋfiːt] (v.) 戰勝；擊敗
6. **kingdom** [ˋkɪŋdəm] (n.) 王國
7. **take** A **away from** B 將 A 帶離 B
8. **huge** [hjuːdʒ] (a.) 巨大的
9. **trouble** [ˋtrʌbl] (n.) 麻煩的事
10. **attack** [əˋtæk] (v.) 進攻；攻擊
11. **nearby** [ˌnɪrˋbaɪ] (a.) 附近的

27

As soon as Simon left, Tarras came to Ivan's house.

"Dear brother," said Tarras. "Tell me where you got your gold. If I had some money, I could become a successful trader[1]."

Ivan was very surprised. "You should have told me this before. Just follow[2] me."

Ivan made a big pile of[3] gold, and asked Tarras if it was enough.

"Thank you, Ivan," said Tarras. "It will be enough for now[4]."

Ivan replied, "If you want more, come back. It is no trouble at all." Tarras took his gold and went away to start his business.

1. **trader** [ˈtreɪdə(r)] (n.) 商人
2. **follow** [ˈfɑːloʊ] (v.) 跟隨
3. **a pile of** 一堆
4. **for now** 目前

One Point Lesson

◦ **If I had some money, I could become a successful trader.** 只要有一點錢，就能讓我成為成功的商人。

本句為「假設語氣」，是一種表示假設狀態的句型，由「if」所引導的副詞子句，再加上主要子句所構成。

e.g. **If I were a teacher, I could teach you well.**
如果我是老師，可以把你教得很好。

28

This is how Simon became the ruler of a nearby kingdom and Tarras became a wealthy[1] trader. However, the brothers were not satisfied[2].

"I do not have enough money to care for my soldiers," said Simon.

"And I do not have enough soldiers to guard[3] my money," said Tarras.

"Let's go back to Ivan," said Simon.

But Ivan refused. "Simon, I did not know your soldiers would kill so many people. And Tarras, you have purchased[4] all the cows in my village. The people cannot eat gold, so they have no food. I regret[5] helping you before."

The brothers left Ivan, and made new plans[6].

"If I give you some soldiers, then you can give me some money," said Simon.

Tarras agreed, and both the brothers became leaders[7].

Meanwhile[8], Ivan became popular[9] because of his talents[10] and good nature[11]. The people in his kingdom chose[12] him as their ruler.

1. **wealthy** [`welθi] (a.) 富裕的
2. **satisfied** [`sætɪsfaɪd] (a.)
   滿意的；滿足的
3. **guard** [gɑ:rd] (v.) 保衛；看守
4. **purchase** [`pɜ:rtʃəs] (v.) 買
5. **regret** [rɪ`gret] (v.) 後悔
6. **make plans** 制訂計畫
7. **leader** [`li:də(r)] (n.) 領導者
8. **meanwhile** [`mi:nwaɪl] (adv.)
   其間；同時
9. **popular** [`pɑ:pjələ(r)] (a.)
   受歡迎的
10. **talent** [`tælənt] (n.) 才能
11. **nature** [`neɪtʃə(r)] (n.)
    天性；本質
12. **choose** [tʃu:z] (v.) 選擇
    (choose-chose-chosen)

29

The old Devil never heard from[1] his little devils, so he came up to look around. He saw that the three brothers were successful and happy. This made him very angry. He decided he would have to ruin the brothers himself.

He first went to Simon disguised as[2] a great general. He showed Simon how to make his army more powerful[3]. Then the Devil told Simon that he could defeat India.

Soon Simon's armies were marching against[4] India again. But he didn't know that the Devil had given the king of India a flying machine[5]. This machine dropped[6] bombs[7] on Simon's armies.

Simon could do nothing about it, and he lost[8] the war. All of Simon's soldiers died, and Simon had to run away[9], again.

1. **hear from** 收到……消息
2. **disguised as** [dɪsˈɡaɪz] 偽裝成
3. **powerful** [ˈpaʊərfl] (a.) 強大的
4. **against** [əˈɡeɪnst] (prep.) 對著
5. **flying machine** 飛機
6. **drop** [drɑːp] (v.) 落下；降下
7. **bomb** [bɑːm] (n.) 炸彈
8. **lose** [luːz] (v.) 輸掉；失敗
9. **run away** 逃跑

Ivan the Fool

Next, the Devil went to Tarras's kingdom.
He pretended to[1] be a very rich merchant[2].
He bought everything at high prices. Soon all
the people wanted to sell their goods[3] to the
Devil.

At first [4], Tarras was happy because he
made money from the taxes[5]. But when Tarras
tried to buy something, he couldn't. All the
merchants wanted to make more money
selling to the Devil. Tarras increased[6] his
offers[7], but the Devil did the same.

Soon, the only business people did with
Tarras was to pay[8] him taxes. Tarras soon
had piles of gold, but he could not even buy
food. Starving[9], Tarras fled[10] his kingdom.

1. **pretend to** 假裝；佯裝
2. **merchant** [ˋmɜːrtʃənt] (n.)
   商人
3. **goods** [gʊdz] (n.) 商品；貨物
4. **at first** 起先
5. **tax** [tæks] (n.) 稅（金）
6. **increase** [ɪnˋkriːs] (v.) 增加
7. **offer** [ˋɔːfə(r)] (n.) 出價
8. **pay** [peɪ] (v.) 支付
9. **starve** [stɑːrv] (v.) 挨餓
10. **flee** [fliː] (v.) 逃走
    (flee-fled-fled)

31

The Devil visited Ivan's kingdom next. He saw that the people there worked hard, but did not have much gold. They worked just enough to live.

The Devil appeared[1] before[2] Ivan, looking like[3] a general.

"Ivan, you should have an army," said the Devil. "I will make your people into a powerful army."

"Very well," said Ivan. "But you must teach them to sing and dance also."

The Devil suggested[4] the young men join the army. He promised them vodka and nice uniforms.

But the young men just laughed. "We have enough vodka[5]," they said. "And we don't need uniforms[6]."

1. **appear** [ə`pɪr] (v.) 出現
2. **before** [bɪ`fɔ:(r)] (prep.) 在……面前
3. **look like** 看起來像……
4. **suggest** [sə`dʒest] (v.) 建議；提議
5. **vodka** [`vɑ:dkə] (n.) 伏特加酒
6. **uniform** [`ju:nɪfɔ:rm] (n.) 制服；軍服

"If you do not join the army, you will be punished[7] with death[8]," said the Devil.

"If we become soldiers, we will die fighting anyway," replied the young men.

"Soldiers may or may not be killed[9]," said the Devil angrily. "But if you do not join, you will certainly be killed!"

The young men went to Ivan. "A general said you would kill us if we did not join your army," they said.

Ivan laughed. "If you do not want to join the army, then don't."

7. **punish** [ˋpʌnɪʃ] (v.) 懲罰；處罰
8. **death** [dɛθ] (n.) 死亡
9. **killed** [kɪld] (a.) 被殺死的

32

The old Devil became furious[1]. He became friends with[2] the king of a nearby country called Tarkania.

The Devil told this king that Ivan's land would be easy to take[3]. The Tarkanian king decided to attack.

But when the soldiers arrived in Ivan's kingdom, nobody fought them. Instead, Ivan's people offered[4] them food and drinks[5].

The soldiers told their king, "We will not fight for you anymore. The people here are very friendly[6] and peaceful[7]. We want to live with them."

The Tarkanian king could do nothing. He returned[8] to his kingdom alone. The old Devil was even more upset[9]. Everything he tried against Ivan failed.

1. **furious** [ˋfjʊriəs] (a.) 狂怒的
2. **become friends with**
   與⋯⋯成為朋友
3. **take** [teɪk] (v.) 奪取；佔領
4. **offer** [ˋɔ:fə(r)] (v.) 給予；提供
5. **food and drinks** 飲食
6. **friendly** [ˋfrendli] (a.)
   友好的；親切的
7. **peaceful** [ˋpi:sfl] (a.)
   愛好和平的
8. **return** [rɪˋtɜ:rn] (v.) 返回
9. **upset** [ʌpˋset] (a.) 苦惱的

The Devil decided to try one more time. He disguised himself as a nobleman[1].

He came to Ivan and said, "I want to teach you wisdom[2]."

"Very well," said Ivan. "You may live with us."

The next day, the Devil appeared in the village.

"Listen to me, common people[3]," said the Devil. "Build me a house and I will pay you gold."

The people were amazed to see shiny[4] gold coins. They started to build a house for the Devil.

1. **nobleman** [ˋnoʊblmən] (n.) 貴族
2. **wisdom** [ˋwɪzdəm] (n.) 智慧;才智
3. **common people** 普通人
4. **shiny** [ˋʃaɪni] (a.) 閃耀的
5. **trade** A **for** B 用 A 交換 B
6. **jewelry** [ˋdʒuːəlri] (n.) 珠寶
7. **deal with** 與……做生意
8. **confused** [kənˋfjuːzd] (a.) 困惑的
9. **wound** [wuːnd] (v.) 傷害

Chapter Three
Ivan, the Leader

The farmers traded food for gold[5].
The people used the gold to make jewelry [6] for
the women and toys for the children. However,
they soon had all the gold they wanted. Suddenly,
the people stopped dealing with[7] the nobleman.

The Devil was confused[8]. He went to many
houses, offering gold for food.

"If you offer us something else, we would
trade," they said. "Or if you ask us to help you in
Christ's name, we would give you something."

But the Devil only had gold and just hearing
Christ's name wounded[9] him.

● But the Devil only had gold and just **hearing** Christ's
name wounded him.
但惡魔只有黃金，而且光是聽到基督的名字就會受傷。

動名詞：動詞後面加 -ing，就會變成名詞。此句的 hearing
是主詞。

e.g. **Learning** English is difficult but interesting.
學英文雖然難，但是很有趣。

Finally, the Devil went to Ivan's house. He was starving. Ivan invited the Devil for supper. Ivan's sister served the food.

But in Ivan's kingdom, people with rough[1], dark, hard-working[2] hands were served first. Those with soft, white hands were not served[3] at all. These people had to wait for[4] any food that was left.

Of course, the nobleman's hands were soft and white, with long fingernails[5]. When Ivan's sister saw them, she pushed the Devil away[6].

Ivan said, "Do not be offended[7]. This is our law[8]."

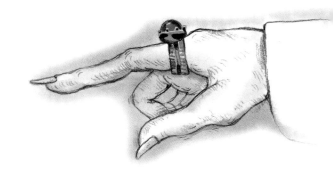

"Do you think people only work with their hands?" asked the nobleman angrily. "You are a fool. Much hard work is done by people who use their heads." Ivan was very impressed[9].

The Devil told Ivan that he would teach Ivan's people how to work with their heads.

The next day, the Devil climbed[10] a tall tower[11] and spoke to the people. Many common folk[12] had come to hear him speak. But they did not understand him.

They waited to see him do work with his head, but all he did was talk.

1. **rough** [rʌf] (a.) 粗糙的
2. **hard-working** [hɑːrd `wɜːrkɪŋ] (a.) 勤勉的
3. **serve** [sɜːrv] (v.) 供應；端上（飯菜）
4. **wait for** 等待
5. **fingernail** [`fɪŋgərneɪl] (n.) 手指甲
6. **push away** 推開
7. **be offended** 被冒犯
8. **law** [lɔː] (n.) 法律
9. **impress** [ɪm`pres] (v.) 給予深刻印象
10. **climb** [klaɪm] (v.) 爬；攀登
11. **tower** [`taʊə(r)] (n.) 塔；高樓
12. **folk** [foʊk] (n.) 人們

99

Finally, the Devil was so weak from hunger[1] that he fell. As he fell, a rope[2] caught[3] around his leg. The Devil's body swung from side to side[4]. His head bumped against[5] the wall of the tower. People said, "Finally! The nobleman is doing work with his head!"

Ivan saw the devil and said, "Well, that is a hard way to do work. It's better to make your hands rough than bump your head."

1. **hunger** [ˋhʌŋgə(r)] (n.)
   挨餓；飢餓
2. **rope** [roʊp] (n.) 繩；索
3. **catch** [kætʃ] (v.) 鉤住
   (catch-caught-caught)
4. **from side to side** 左右的

5. **bump against** 撞到
6. **moment** [ˋmoʊmənt] (n.)
   片刻；瞬間
7. **break** [breɪk] (v.) 斷裂；破碎
8. **fall down** 跌下

At that moment[6], the rope broke[7] and the Devil fell down[8]. Ivan ran to the nobleman, but saw a large Devil lying on the ground. "In the name of our Lord, what is this?" said Ivan. The Devil disappeared, leaving a small hole in the ground.

Ivan still lives and many people come to his kingdom. There is one law that never changes in Ivan's kingdom. Men who have rough, hard-working hands are always given food.

One Point Lesson

◆ Men **who** have rough, hard-working hands are always given food. 努力工作到雙手粗糙的人，總是有飯吃。

關係代名詞 **who**：先行詞是人時，用 who 所引導的子句，來修飾前面的先行詞

e.g. I know the boy **who** is singing on the stage.
我認識在舞台上唱歌的少年。

A Match.

1. destroy •   • a hurt
2. flee •   • b run away
3. disguise •   • c exchange
4. trade •   • d ruin
5. wound •   • e hide

B Rearrange the following sentences in chronological order.

1. The Devil tried to teach Ivan's people how to work with their heads.
2. The Devil tried to make Ivan's people greedy by giving them gold.
3. The Devil told the Tarkanian king he could take Ivan's country.
4. The Devil told young men in Ivan's country to join the army.

_____ ⇨ _____ ⇨ _____ ⇨ _____

Appendixes

1 Basic Grammar

要增強英文閱讀理解能力，應練習找出英文的主結構。
要擁有良好的英語閱讀能力，首先要理解英文的段落結構。

英文的閱讀理解從「分解文章」開始

英文的文章是以「有意義的詞組」（指帶有意義的語句）所構成的。用（／）符號來區別各個意義語塊，請試著掌握其中的意義。

He knew / that she told a lie / at the party.

他知道　　　　　她說了謊　　　　　在舞會上

⇨ 他知道她在舞會上說謊的事。

As she was walking / in the garden, / she smelled /

當她行走　　　　　　在花園　　　　　她聞到味道

something wet.

某樣東西濕濕的

⇨ 她走在花園時聞到潮溼的味道。

一篇文章，要分成幾個有意義的詞組？

可放入（／）符號來區隔有意義詞組的地方，一般是在（1）「主詞＋動詞」之後；（2）and 和 but 等連接詞之前；（3）that、who 等關係代名詞之前；（4）副詞子句的前後，會用（／）符號來區隔。初學者可能在一篇文章中畫很多（／）符號，但隨著閱讀實力的提升，（／）會減少。時間一久，在不太複雜的文章中即使不畫（／）符號，也能一眼就理解整句的意義。

使用（／）符號來閱讀理解英語篇章

1. 能熟悉英文的句型和構造。
2. 可加速閱讀速度。

該方法對於需要邊聽理解的英文聽力也有很好的效果。

從現在開始，早日丟棄過去理解文章的習慣吧！

以直接閱讀理解的方式，重新閱讀《托爾斯泰短篇小說》

從原文中摘錄一小段。以具有意義的詞組將文章做斷句區分，重新閱讀並做理解練習。

Once / there lived a Russian farmer / who had three sons / : Simon, Tarras and Ivan.
很久以前／一位俄羅斯的農夫　　　／有三個兒子／西門、泰瑞斯、伊凡

Simon became a soldier, / and Tarras became a businessman.
西門成為一位軍人　　　／泰瑞斯成為一位商人

Ivan stayed on the farm / and worked hard / for his family.
伊凡留在農地　　　　／勤奮地工作　　／為他的家庭

Simon was very successful.
西門的事業非常成功

The Russian king, / called "Czar", / gave him a large farm.
俄羅斯國王　　　　／稱為沙皇　　／賜給他一大片農田

However, / his wife spent / all their money and more.
然而　　　／他的妻子花掉了／他們所有的財產甚至更多

Simon went to his father.
西門去找他的父親

The Devil was disappointed / to hear about Ivan and his brothers.
魔鬼很失望　　　　　　　／對於聽到西門和他的兄弟們

He wanted people to argue.
他希望人們爭吵

So / the Devil called three young devils / to him.
所以／　魔鬼召喚了三隻小魔鬼　　／到他面前

"I want you / to make Ivan and his brothers fight / with each other," /
said the Devil.
我要你們　／　讓伊凡和他的兄弟爭吵　　　／彼此／
魔鬼說

Can you make them do this?"
你們可以造成他們爭吵嗎？

"Yes, master," / they said.
是的，主人　／他們說

"We will make each brother fail / in his work.
我們會讓每一個兄弟失敗　　／在工作上

Then / they will all go back / to their father's farm / and argue."
然後／他們會回家　　　／到他們父親的田地／並且爭吵

The little devils agreed / that they would each ruin one brother.
小魔鬼們同意 / 他們分別讓一個兄弟破產

Whoever finished first / would then help / the others.
無論誰先做完 / 就去幫助 / 其他人

The next day, / Ivan returned to his field / to finish the plowing.
第二天 / 伊凡回到他的田地 / 要完成耕地的作業

He still had / a terrible stomachache.
他還是有著 / 嚴重的肚子痛

But / Ivan was a strong man, / and he was used to / working every day.
但是 / 伊凡是強壯的人 / 而且他已習慣 / 每天工作

He tried to pick up / his plow that he left / in the ground / last night.
他試著拾起 / 他留下的犁 / 在地上 / 昨晚

It would not move.
它一動也不動

In fact, / the third devil was in the ground / holding it.
實際上 / 第三個小魔鬼在地下 / 抓住它

The devil's legs were wrapped / around the plow.
小魔鬼的雙腿圍住 / 繞著犁

Ivan put his hand / in the ground.
伊凡把他的手 / 伸進地底

He felt something soft.
他摸到柔軟的東西

With his great strength, / he pulled it out.
以他極大的力量 / 他將它拉出來

2

Guide to Listening Comprehension

 When listening to the story, use some of the techniques shown below. If you take time to study some phonetic characteristics of English, listening will be easier.

Get in the flow of English.

English creates a rhythm formed by combinations of strong and weak stress intonations. Each word has its particular stress that combines with other words to form the overall pattern of stress or rhythm in a particular sentence.

When you are speaking and listening to English, it is essential to get in the flow of the rhythm of English. It takes a lot of practice to get used to such a rhythm. So, you need to start by identifying the stressed syllable in a word.

Listen for the strongly stressed words and phrases.

In English, key words and phrases that are essential to the meaning of a sentence are stressed louder. Therefore, pay attention to the words stressed with a higher pitch. When listening to an English recording for the first time, what matters most is to listen for a general understanding of what you hear. Do not try to hear every single word. Most of the unstressed words are articles or auxiliary verbs, which don't play an important role in the general context. At this level, you can ignore them.

Pay attention to liaisons.

In reading English, words are written with a space between them. There isn't such an obvious guide when it comes to listening to English. In oral English, there are many cases when the sounds of words are linked with adjacent words.

For instance, let's think about the phrase "**take off**," which can be used in "take off your clothes." "Take off your clothes" doesn't sound like [teɪk ɔːf] with each of the words completely and clearly separated from the others. Instead, it sounds as if almost all the words in context are slurred together, [ˈteɪkɔːf], for a more natural sound.

Shadow the voice of the native speaker.

Finally, you need to mimic the voice of the native speaker. Once you are sure you know how to pronounce all the words in a sentence, try to repeat them like an echo. Listen to the book again, but this time you should try a fun exercise while listening to the English.

This exercise is called "shadowing." The word "shadow" means a dark shade that is formed on a surface. When used as a verb, the word refers to the action of following someone or something like a shadow. In this exercise, pretend you are a parrot and try to shadow the voice of the native speaker.

Try to mimic the reader's voice by speaking at the same speed, with the same strong and weak stresses on words, and pausing or stopping at the same points.

Experts have already proven this technique to be effective. If you practice this shadowing exercise, your English speaking and listening skills will improve by leaps and bounds. While shadowing the native speaker, don't forget to pay attention to the meaning of each phrase and sentence.

Step 1 Listen to what you want to shadow many times. Start out by just trying to shadow a few words or a sentence.

 Step 2 Mimic the CD out loud. You can shadow everything the speaker says as if you are singing a round, or you also can speak simultaneously with the recorded voice of the native speaker.

 Step 3 As you practice more, try to shadow more. For instance, shadow a whole sentence or paragraph instead of just a few words.

3 Listening Guide

以下為《托爾斯泰短篇小說》各章節的前半部。一開始若能聽清楚發音，之後就沒有聽力的負擔。先聽過摘錄的章節，之後再反覆聆聽括弧內單字的發音，並仔細閱讀各種發音的說明。

以下都是以英語的典型發音為基礎，所做的簡易說明，即使這裡未提到的發音，也可以配合音檔反覆聆聽，如此一來聽力必能更上層樓。

Chapter One page 16　

In old Russia, there was once an old shoemaker named Simon. He and his wife were not rich. One day in the (**❶**) (　　　), Simon left his house to buy a winter coat. He and his wife needed a new coat to share.

He had only three rubles but he also (**❷**) (　　　) visit some of his customers on the way. They owed him five rubles for work he had already done.

❶ late fall: late 的 [t] 音，像前音的尾音一樣發出聲音來。

❷ planned to: planned 最後的 [d] 音與 to 連在一起發音，聽起來像只有一個音。當相同或相似的音連接在一起時，通常聽起來像只有一個音。

After one year, a rich (❶) came to Simon's shop.
He asked, "Who is the master shoemaker here?"
"I am, sir," said Simon. "How can I help you?"
The rich gentleman showed Simon a large (❷)
(   ) very fine leather.
"Do you know (❸) (   ) (   ) leather this is?"
"It's good leather, sir," said Simon.

❶ **gentleman:** 重音在第一音節。-nt- 連在一起發，[t] 音常會被擺在不同音節。internet 的發音也有相同的情況。

❷ **piece of:** 像一個單字般連在一起發音，聽起來像一個單字，of 常會變成連音或聽不出 [v] 的發音。

❸ **what kind of:** 常出現的片語，請把發音也當一個單字熟記起來。這類發音隨著上下文會發出不同的語調型態，且其中 kind 的 [d] 音聽起來為另一個音節的發音。

Once there lived a (❶) farmer who had three sons: Simon, Tarras and Ivan.
Simon became a soldier, and Tarras (❷) (   ) businessman. Ivan stayed on the farm and worked hard for his family.

❶ **Russian:** 外來語或專有名詞，常因為我們依照母語的習慣來發音，所以造成許多聽力上的困難。即使是已知道的外來語，也要養成注意其發音和重音的習慣。

❷ **became a:** 兩個單字連在一起發音，因此聽起來像是一個單字，became 的重音在第二音節。

Chapter Two page 66 🎧 39

After finishing his mission, the first devil (❶) (   ) Ivan's farm. However, he (❷) not find his brother.
"Something (❸) (   ) happened to my brother. I will have to stop Ivan myself," said the first devil, seeing the small hole in the ground.

① **went to:** went to 要連在一起唸，在英語中若相同的音連在一起只需發音一次。

② **could:** 助動詞幾乎無法發完整的音，最後的 [d] 音常聽不到。

③ **must have:** 在一段文字中，常快速發音，同時是發出弱音帶過。have 的 [h] 音會與前一個單字變成連音，而 must 的 [t] 音亦變得不清楚甚至於省略。

Chapter Three page 82 🎧40

The (**①**) (   ), Simon was knocking on Ivan's door.
"Brother, tell me where the soldiers came from,"
Simon (**②**).
"I will show you," said Ivan. He took Simon into the barn and made some soldiers from straw.
"This is (**③**)!" said Simon.

① **next morning:** -xt 發 [st] 的音，且 [t] 的音常省略不發出來。

② **asked:** 過去式 -ed 前面若是緊接著 [p]、[k]、[f]、[s] 等子音，會發 [t] 音。

③ **amazing:** 重音在第二音節，相對的在重音節周圍的音聽起來 s 會變得微弱。特別是當重音在第二音節，而第一音節是母音時，第一音節會被忽略而聽不出發音。

Listening Comprehension

  A Listen to the CD and match each description to the right character.

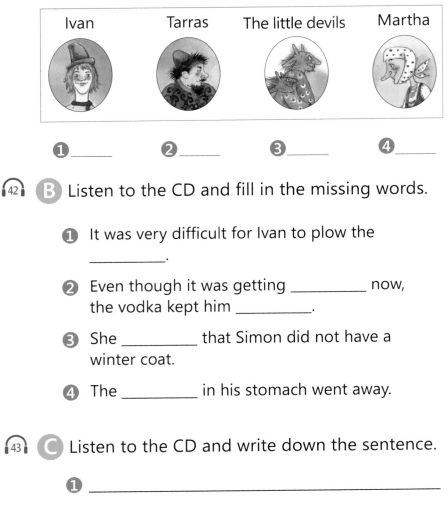

Ivan   Tarras   The little devils   Martha

❶ _____   ❷ _____   ❸ _____   ❹ _____

42 **B** Listen to the CD and fill in the missing words.

❶ It was very difficult for Ivan to plow the
_____.

❷ Even though it was getting _____ now,
the vodka kept him _____.

❸ She _____ that Simon did not have a
winter coat.

❹ The _____ in his stomach went away.

43 **C** Listen to the CD and write down the sentence.

❶ _____

❷ _____

🎧 44 **D** Choose the correct answer.

❶ _____?

   (a) It is better to try and accomplish great things than to live simply.

   (b) Lazy people don't get enough to eat.

   (c) A simple life of hard work is the best way to live.

❷ _____?

   (a) You should believe that God would live in you.

   (b) Men do not know when they will die, so they make foolish plans.

   (c) Men have much to learn from angels.

🎧 45 **E** Listen to the CD and write down the sentences. Rearrange the sentences in chronological order.

❶ _____

❷ _____

❸ _____

❹ _____

❺ _____

❻ _____

_____ ⇨ _____ ⇨ _____ ⇨ _____ ⇨ _____ ⇨ _____

列夫‧尼古拉耶維奇‧托爾斯泰（Lev Nikolayevich Tolstoy, 1828–1910）是俄國最傑出的作家，並被認為世上最偉大的哲學家。托爾斯泰生於貴族地主家庭，為家中第四位男孩。大學輟學後，他返鄉繼承家業，並試圖改善家中封建土地上農民的生活。

然而，實現理想之路失敗後，他過著混沌的日子。1857 年，他加入軍隊，從事軍事活動。

這段期間，戰爭的體驗轉化為提筆的動力，他在許多著作中皆透露了生死、種族議題與屠殺的全面洞見。

1855 年結束軍旅生活前，他已以新星之姿廣受文壇認可。1862 年結婚後，他開始專注於寫作，重要作品有《戰爭與和平》（War and Peace）、《安娜‧卡列尼娜》（Anna Karenina）和《復活》（Resurrection）。

他寫作的共通主題有普世的愛、善惡價值、信仰與懷疑，以及死亡與人生的意義。托爾斯泰以特有的說服力，用易懂並值得玩味的方式處理這些主題。

在 82 年的生命裡，他撰寫將近 90 部作品，與杜斯妥也夫斯基（Dostoyevsky）被公認為俄國最偉大的小說家。

Lev Tolstoy in Yasnaya Polyana, 1908, the first color photo portrait in Russia

　　《人靠什麼活下去》與《傻子伊凡》是托爾斯泰的短篇代表作。

　　《人靠什麼活下去》反映出托爾斯泰對宗教的個人觀點。藉由大天使米迦勒在人世的經歷，托爾斯泰提出人靠什麼而活的問題，並給了他的答案：人藉著愛活下去。

　　《傻子伊凡》（1885）的故事以民間傳說的形式寫成，描述天真、誠實、勤勞的伊凡由於辛勤工作，勝過他兩個粗俗貪心的哥哥，並獲得成功。在故事裡，托爾斯泰以清晰簡單的方式，描述「傻子伊凡」所體現完美的人類特質。

　　閱讀托爾斯泰的短篇故事為一享受，它能引發讀者真誠而詳實地省思自己的生命。故事簡單巧妙地描寫關於責任、愛與友情等議題，以及平凡百姓日常生活的勞動所具的神聖性。

人靠什麼活下去

p. 14-15 **人物簡介**

Simon 西門

我是一個純樸的鞋匠，住在俄國鄉間。因為賺錢不易，生活十分困苦，我和妻子馬大努力工作，想盡量過上好一點的日子。然而，在我遇到了一個全身一絲不掛的年輕人後，我們的生活起了一點變化。

Michael 大天使米迦勒

我是來自天堂的天使，上帝要我來召集善人死後的靈魂，引領他們回天堂。有一次，我不想帶一位母親的靈魂回天堂，上帝就要我去西門家住，好讓我了解上帝給人類的旨意。

Martha 馬大

我是西門的妻子。西門大多時候是個老好人，但他有時候會讓我很生氣。舉例來說，他在工作上應該強悍一點，因為他老是讓客人的帳拖欠很久！

Rich Gentleman 豪紳

我是富裕的貴族，買得起歐洲最精品的東西！我有一些當官的朋友，如果有人敢違逆我的意思，我就能他們嚐到後果！

Woman who raises two daughters 育有兩女的婦女

鄰居一對夫婦去世，留下兩個女兒。我們把他們的女兒收養下來，視如己出，當親生骨肉一樣。

[第一章] 鞋匠西門

p. 16–17 很久以前,在俄羅斯有一位老鞋匠,叫做西門,他和妻子兩人生活貧困。

深秋的一天,西門出門要去買一件新冬裘,讓夫妻兩人輪流穿來過冬。

西門身上只有三盧布,他打算沿路上去客戶家收款,他還有五盧布的工錢沒收齊。

他訪了幾家客戶,只收到了二十戈比左右。

鞋匠走進商店,但不夠錢買大衣,他問老闆是否可以先付部分的錢,剩下的下次再付。

老闆卻回道:「把錢一次帶齊吧,我們都知道,賒帳的錢是很難收的。」

p. 18 西門感到十分沮喪。他把收到的二十戈比拿去買了伏特加,然後走回家。天色漸暗了,但體內的伏特加還能讓他感到暖和。

西門一路走著,當他途經一間小教堂時,看到教堂後面有一個白白的東西,看起來像是一個沒穿衣服全身赤裸的人!西門心頭一驚。

他心想:「一定是強盜殺掉了他,把他的衣服給扒走了。我得趕快離開,免得也遇上強盜了!」

p. 20–21 西門趕緊離開教堂。沒多久,他回頭看。

西門心忖道:「該怎麼辦才好?我要是回去看他,搞不好他會對我謀衣害命。況且就算他不會對我怎樣,我又能幫得上什麼忙呢?」

於是西門繼續往前走，直到看不見身後的那個人。

走到下一個斜坡頂時，他突然停下來。

「我在做什麼呀？」他想：「那個人可能會死啊！我真是應該覺得慚愧啊！」於是他回頭往教堂方向走去。

當他走到教堂後面時，他看到一個年輕人。這個年輕人長得高大，身強體健的，但一臉害怕的模樣。

他長相英俊，面容親切。西門霎時就喜歡上了這年輕人，他脫下自己的舊外套，把它披在年輕人肩上。西門手上還有一雙靴子，就把靴子也給了年輕人。

p. 22–23 「你能走嗎？」西門問。

年輕人站起來，親切地望著西門，一句話也沒說。

「你為什麼不說話？你從哪裡來的？」西門問。

年輕人口氣溫和，靜靜地答道：「我不是這附近的人。」

西門說：「我想也是，這附近的人我都認識。那你怎麼會來這裡啊？」

「我無可奉告。」年輕人回答：「我只能說，這是上帝給我的懲罰。」

西門說：「喔，當然啦，上帝統治所有人類。如果你沒有地方可去，那你可以跟我一起回家，這樣起碼可以讓你暖和一點。」

西門一路帶著陌生人回家，心裡頭卻很擔心妻子的反應。

妻子馬大聽到西門回到家的聲音，也聞到伏特加的味道，還留意到西門沒有買回冬裘。

「他帶回來的這個陌生人是誰？」馬大想：「在酒吧遇到的另一個酒鬼？」馬大失望透了。

p. 24–25 西門説：「馬大，晚餐要是弄好了，我們就開飯吧！」

馬大氣呼呼地説道：「你太晚回來了，我沒準備晚餐！你不但回來晚了，也沒帶大衣回來！你把錢都拿去買伏特加，還帶了個陌生人回家，他甚至連衣服都沒穿！像你們這樣的酒鬼別想有晚餐啦！」

「馬大，妳説夠了。」西門想解釋，但妻子正在氣頭上。

她又説道：「我當初根本就不該嫁給你，沒有大衣，我們怎麼過冬啊？你什麼都不會，只會把酒鬼帶回家，要跟我們分那麼一丁點的食物！」

馬大瞄了陌生人一眼，繼續説道：「他要是一個正派的人，怎麼會一絲不掛？你告訴我，他是從哪兒來的？」

「我本來就想告訴妳的啊！」西門説。於是他就把遇見年輕人的經過告訴妻子。

馬大聽著，一邊打量著年輕人。年輕人坐在長凳的一頭，一動也不動。他雙手擱在大腿上，望著地板，一副可憐樣。

p. 26–27 西門解釋完之後，説道：「馬大，難道妳不愛上帝嗎？」

馬大聽他這麼一問，心也就軟了下來。她轉身去廚房拿了茶和麵包，拿到陌生人面前。

「吃吧！想吃就吃吧！」她説。

馬大看著陌生人吃東西，心頭的氣也消了，心想這年輕人是能討她喜歡的。

陌生人突然抬起頭，笑了笑，臉上散發出一道光芒，說道：「謝謝妳。」

陌生人留了下來，跟西門學做鞋子，他學得很快，手很巧。他只告訴西門夫婦，說他叫米迦勒。米迦勒的鞋子做得很好，很多人來找他做鞋子。不多久，西門和馬大就不愁沒錢買食物和衣服了。

p. 30–31 天上來的人：天使

在本故事中，拜訪西門和馬大這對夫婦的那位天使米迦勒，是眾天使之首。早在上帝創造人類之前，上帝就創造了天使。

天使的外表與人類無異，但長著一對白色的大翅膀，通常都穿著潔白光亮的長袍。事實上，人類無法直視天使的臉孔，因為他們的頭和身體似乎會發出光芒。

天使是上帝的僕人，他們主要的任務是向人類傳達上帝的旨意。

天使會對人們示現上帝的愛，並盡力幫助人們。天使還有一個工作是帶領亡靈返回天堂，他們會在善人臨終後，引領其靈魂上天堂。

有時，天使也會保護人們，像是在發生嚴重意外時拯救人類。也因此，人們在危難時，會向「守護天使」祈求幫助。

[第二章] 人間的天使

p. 32–33 一年後，一位有錢的貴族豪紳來到西門的鞋店，問道：「誰是這家鞋店的大師傅？」

「我是，先生。」西門說：「需要我為您服務嗎？」

豪紳拿出一大塊上好的皮革給西門看。

「你知道這是什麼皮嗎？」

「先生，這是一塊好皮革。」西門回答。

豪紳笑道：「你這個笨蛋啊，這可是最上等的皮革呢。我要你幫我做一雙靴子，而且要能穿上一年也不會壞。你做得出來嗎？」

西門很惶恐，他看看米迦勒，問道：「我們該接下這份工作嗎？」

米迦勒點點頭，眼神像是對著豪紳的背後望去，但豪紳的背後並沒有人，米迦勒又突然微笑了起來。

「你在笑什麼啊，傻蛋？」豪紳吼道：「你最好現在就開始幹活，我兩天後來拿！」

p. 34　隔天，米迦勒開始製作豪紳的靴子。當西門去察看他工作時，驚訝地叫了出來。

「你在做什麼啊？」西門喊道：「你做的是便鞋，不是靴子啊！」

就在這時，門外響起了敲門聲。西門打開門，看到豪紳的僕人。

僕人說道：「夫人為了靴子的事，派我來找你。」

西門感到一陣害怕。

僕人繼續說：「主人用不到靴子了，他人已經過世了，夫人希望您能為他的喪禮製作一雙便鞋。」

西門很詫異。米迦勒不出聲息地拿起他做好的便鞋，交給僕人。僕人躬了身說道：「謝謝您，鞋師傅。」

p. 36–37　轉眼，米迦勒來西門家已經有六年之久了。一天，米迦勒站在窗邊，凝視著窗外。西門覺得很奇怪，因為米迦勒向來對外面的世界興趣缺缺。

「你看！」馬大說：「有一個婦人往我們這裡走來，她帶著兩個女兒，其中一個女兒的一隻腳跛了。」

婦人走進鞋匠的店裡。西門說：「您好，需要我們為您服務嗎？」

「我想為這兩個女孩做雙皮鞋。」婦人說道。

「這我們可以做到。」西門說著注意到米迦勒正盯著小女孩瞧。

「這小女孩的腳是怎麼弄傷的啊？」西門問：「是天生的嗎？」

婦人答道：「不是，是她母親弄傷的。我不是她們的親生母親，她們是我鄰居的孩子，一對雙胞胎，六年前左右出生的。她們父親在她們出生前一星期過世，母親生下她們之後，也走了。她死的時候，身體壓到女兒，把她的腿給扭傷了。

我當時因為也剛生過產，所以有奶水可以餵她們。我自己的孩子後來不幸夭折，於是我就撫養這兩個女孩，現在我對她們是視如己出。」

p. 38–39 馬大說：「的確，沒有父母，人還可以存活下來，但要是沒有上帝，人就活不下來了。」

這時，一道光芒突然照亮了整個房間。大家望向米迦勒，因為光芒是從他那裡發射出來的。他抬頭望著天上，一臉微笑。

他放下手上的工具，脫下圍裙，向西門和馬大躬了身。

「上帝已經原諒我了。」他說，「很遺憾我得離開你們，我得走了。」

西門對米迦勒說：「現在，我親眼見到你不是凡夫，我是留不住你的，但如果可以的話，請告訴我你的來歷吧。」

米迦勒對西門笑了笑。

他說道：「我最少是應該解釋一下的。六年前，我因為違背上帝的旨意而受到懲罰，祂當時派我去引領一個婦女的靈魂，那位婦女就是剛剛那對雙胞胎的親生母親。

當時我到她家時，看到了那兩個新生兒。她們的母親懇求我不要帶走她的靈魂，所以我就返回天堂，請求上帝拯救她。」

p. 40–41「上帝告訴我，『回去帶回母親的靈魂，接下來你還得學三個真理。第一，學習什麼活在人類心中；第二，學習人類缺乏什麼；第三，學習人是靠什麼活下去的。等你學到這三件事之後，你就可以返回天堂。』

於是，我飛回婦人的屋子，帶走她的靈魂，然後我就突然失去我的翅膀，掉落到了人間。接著，西門，你發現了我，我那時一絲不掛地在教堂後面打著哆嗦。

我又孤獨又害怕，以為你不會幫助我，但你走回來，把你的衣服給了我！

然後，我和你走回家，馬大那時候看起來很生氣，我很害怕，但她還是憐憫了我，把你們僅有的一點食物給了我。當時我一陣微笑，因為我學到了上帝的第一個真理：愛，活在人類的心中。」

p. 42–43「一年之後，那位豪紳來找我們，我看到他身後站了死亡天使，他已經命在旦夕，卻想要一雙能穿得上一年的靴子，於是我了解了人類所欠缺的是什麼：人類不知道自己真正需要的是什麼。我那時也笑了，因為我學到了第二個真理。

就在剛才，那婦人來時，我學到了第三個真理。她真心愛兩個小女孩，即使她們不是她親生的骨肉，我因此看到了上帝在她心中，於是我明白了人類是靠著愛而活下去的，所以我這一次我又笑了。」

米迦勒的身形變得越來越高大，全身散發閃亮的光芒，讓西門與馬大無法直視。他的身體長出翅膀，講話的聲音變大，語調也轉為堅定。

「我現在明白，人僅是靠著愛而活下來的。有愛，便與上帝同在，上帝就在他心中，因為，上帝就是愛。」

接著，鞋店的屋頂被打開，一道光芒自天上降下。米迦勒揮動翅膀，向著光飛去。西門和馬大用手遮住兩眼，跪在地上。等西門再張開眼時，屋頂已經闔上，店裡頭除了他和馬大，別無他人。

傻子伊凡

p. 48–49 人物簡介

Ivan 伊凡

我名叫伊凡，是俄羅斯的一個農夫。人們說我是傻子，但我無所謂啦，我只想每天都努力幹活工作，賺足夠的錢養家。

Simon 西門

我叫西門，是全俄羅斯最偉大的軍人，我帶領的軍隊叱吒沙場！然而，在我與印度對戰時，魔鬼使詐設計了我。

Tarras 泰瑞斯

我是泰瑞斯，俄羅斯最富有的商人！好吧，至少在魔鬼打擊我的事業之前，我很富有。不過現在呢，我住在伊凡家。

The Devil 魔鬼

我是魔鬼，最喜歡讓人們起聲色貨利之貪念！只是，我卻動不了伊凡！伊凡的頭腦太簡單了，讓我很傷腦筋啊！

The little Devils 小鬼惡魔

我們是小鬼兄弟，謹遵魔鬼的指示行事。毀掉人們的生活，是我們的樂趣！西門和泰瑞斯根本不是我們的對手，伊凡呢，他冥頑不靈得過頭又單純！他把我們逮住之後，硬要我們拿出什麼東西來給他。要是被魔鬼給瞧見了，我們就吃不完兜著走！

﹝第一章﹞魔鬼的計畫

p. 50–51 從前俄羅斯有一位農夫，他有三個兒子，分別是西門、泰瑞斯和伊凡。西門是一位軍人，泰瑞斯在做生意，伊凡在家鄉務農，努力種田，養家活口。

西門戰功彪炳，俄羅斯的國王，我們稱為「沙皇」，賜給他一大片農地，然而卻被妻子揮霍殆盡，他只得回家向父親開口。

西門說：「親愛的爸爸，我是您的兒子，把我的那份財產給我吧。」

父親卻答道：「這對伊凡和妹妹不公平，是他們的努力，我們才有這一切的。」

西門說：「伊凡是個傻子，妹妹是個啞巴，他們根本不需要錢。」

父親說：「那你去問伊凡，看他怎麼說！」

伊凡的回答是：「好啊，那就讓他拿走他的份吧！」

p. 52–53 沒多久，另一個哥哥泰瑞斯也回來了。他對父親說：「西門拿走了他那一份財產，那我呢？」

父親也拒絕道：「你啊，就跟西門一樣，沒為我們的田地出過力。」

於是泰瑞斯找伊凡說：「給我你一半的收成和一匹馬就好了。」

伊凡回答：「好啊，拿走你應得的份。」泰瑞斯拿到索求的東西後便離開了。

聽到伊凡和哥哥們的事，魔鬼覺得很沒勁。魔鬼想看的就是人們的紛爭。

於是，他就招來三個小鬼惡魔，說道：「我要你們去讓伊凡三兄弟起內鬨，這你們辦得到吧？」

小鬼們回答：「遵命，主子！我們會讓他們三兄弟一敗塗地，回來爭著分家產。」

p. 54 小鬼們決定兵分三路，準備將三兄弟各個擊破，先完成任務的小鬼，就去支援其他的小鬼。

一個月後，第一個完成任務的小鬼回報工作。

「我已經大功告成了！」他很神氣地說：「明天，西門就會回去找父親了。首先我先煽動西門鼓起勇氣去稟見沙皇，說他可以攻下印度。沙皇於是就任命他為主帥，前進沙場。

接著，我飛去找印度國王，教他如何把稻草變成士兵。這些草兵草將，殺敵不少呢。

沙皇非常震怒，下令把西門關進地牢，準備明天就處決他。不過呢，我今晚會幫他逃獄的啦。現在，兄弟們，你們哪一位需要我來支援呢？」

p. 56–57 第二個小鬼說：「我才不需要呢！我下星期就可以把泰瑞斯搞定了。我把他變得更加貪心不滿，讓他看到什麼就買，傾家蕩產！不消多久，他就會一無所有，回家找老爸了。」

第三個小鬼一臉困窘，說道：「我啊，諸事不順。我在伊凡早上喝的茶杯裡頭吐了口水，想讓他肚子痛，可是他還是起了床，去田裡耕種。

接著，我把土地變得很硬，伊凡犁起田來，就會寸步難行。如此這般，我想他應該就會索性不犁田了，結果他仍照幹！

所以我又鑽入土裡，用手揣住犁刀，結果他賣力一推，就犁掉了我的手指了！」

小鬼嘆了口氣：「來吧！兄弟！你們完成任務後，就來幫我吧！我們得讓伊凡養家不成。」

p. 58-59 第二天，伊凡回到田裡想將田地犁好，雖然他肚子還是很疼，但他很能忍，習慣了每天都要上工。

伊凡想把昨晚擱在田裡的犁拿起來，卻拿不動。原來，是被土裡的第三個小鬼給抓住了，他用兩腿緊緊纏住了犁。

伊凡把手伸進土裡，摸到軟軟的東西，他用力一拔，抓到了一隻醜醜的動物！

伊凡覺得噁心，便舉起手，想將小鬼對準犁刀甩過去。

「不要殺我啊！」小鬼大叫：「你要什麼我都給啊！」

伊凡放下手臂，抓了抓頭，說道：「我的肚子痛得不得了，你能治好嗎？」

小鬼回答：「當然！放了我，我就去找解藥給你！」

p. 60-61 那隻小生物看了看四周，拔起了一把菜根交給
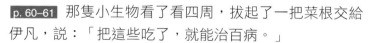
伊凡，說：「把這些吃了，就能治百病。」

伊凡吃了一些菜根之後，肚子就不痛了。伊凡說：「太好了！那你可以走了，上帝保佑你！」

魔鬼們是最痛恨聽到上帝的名字的，所以小鬼立刻溜走，只在地上留了一個小洞。

那天傍晚，伊凡看到了哥哥西門和嫂子坐在餐桌前。西門說：「嘿，伊凡，我現在一無所有回到家裡頭了，你可以在我找到工作前照料我們的生活嗎？」

伊凡回答：「可以啊，你們可以和我們住在一起。」

伊凡坐下後，嫂子對丈夫說：「這樣一個又髒又臭的農夫，我沒辦法跟他一起吃飯啦。」

西門於是對伊凡說：「嫂子受不了你的味道，你可以去陽台吃吧。」

「好啊。」伊凡回答。

p.64–65 另一種天使──魔鬼

魔鬼想讓伊凡一家人貪求財富，而敗盡家業。在基督教的神話裡，這是魔鬼的典型作為。

魔鬼最為人所熟知的事，就是說他很久以前曾是上帝底下的天使長，原名叫路西弗。

路西弗自認為他比上帝更強壯、更偉大，他說服了許多天使加入他們，與上帝對抗。但上帝與祂忠誠的天使，力量才是更強大的，路西弗於是戰敗。

上帝將路西弗和那些反叛的天使逐出天堂，掉進了地獄，這也就是路西弗等一行天使被稱為「墮落天使」的原因了。在他們被逐出天堂時，上帝改變了他們的外型，讓他們長相變得像野獸一樣。

魔鬼們通常被描繪成手上持著長柄叉，他們就是用這些長柄叉來取人們死後的靈魂的。所以，你要是一生行惡，死時就可能看得到魔鬼了喔！

[第二章] 伊凡與小鬼惡魔

p. 66-67 第一個小鬼完成任務之後，便趕到伊凡的農地，但卻沒看到他小鬼兄弟。

「他一定是發生了什麼事，我得獨力來阻撓伊凡了！」小鬼邊說，邊看著地上的小洞。

他先用水淹沒田裡的草，讓伊凡刈草時困難重重。沒多久，伊凡割草就割累了，他自言自語說：「等一下再回來割，不把所有的草割下來，就不歇手。」

小鬼躲在草叢裡，伊凡沒多久就回到田裡來。小鬼趁伊凡揮下鐮刀時，把刀刃末端按入土裡，但伊凡力氣大，很快就把鐮刀拔了出來。小鬼跳開要逃跑，尾巴未料竟被伊凡給割斷。

p. 68-69 那一天裡，小鬼千方百計想阻撓伊凡工作，但伊凡總還是把工作給做完了。

伊凡說道：「這下子可以開始來種燕麥了。」

小鬼心想：「明兒個一定要阻止他！」

第二天，小鬼醒來後，發現伊凡已經在夜裡種了燕麥了！

「他都不用睡覺的喔？」小鬼喃喃自語。

「我得好好想個法子，他很快就會需要用到乾草，在他去穀倉之前，我要先去把他的乾草變爛掉！」

小鬼把乾草弄濕讓它變爛後，便去休息了。

又隔天，伊凡拿著長柄叉來穀倉取乾草。他把叉子插進乾草堆，感覺刺到了什麼硬硬的東西，這時傳來一聲怪叫聲。

叉子上插了一個小鬼！伊凡說：「你不是說你要走了嗎！」

小鬼答道：「那是別人啦，你之前看到的是我兄弟啦！」

p. 70–71 「我不管你是誰了，反正我要把你幹掉。」伊凡説。

「求求你不要啊！」小鬼叫道：「我可以用稻草幫你製造士兵！」

「士兵有什麼用？」伊凡説。

「士兵幾乎可以幫人做任何事。」小鬼回答。

「那你就讓我看看你怎麼製造士兵。」伊凡説。

小鬼將稻草揉成一團，説了幾句咒語，沒多久，穀倉旁就有一群士兵在行軍了！

「現在，讓我走吧！」小鬼説。

伊凡説：「等等，那麼多士兵很耗糧食的，我要怎麼把他們變回稻草？」

「只要説『士兵何其多，稻草何其多』，他們就會消失了！」小鬼説。

伊凡説：「好吧，你可以走了，願上帝保佑你。」伊凡一説完「上帝」，小鬼立刻遁地消失，也在地上留了一個小洞。

p. 73 伊凡回到家，很驚訝地看到二哥泰瑞斯和二嫂。泰瑞斯已經破產，一臉尷尬樣。

「嗨，伊凡，」他説：「在我重新創業之前，我們可以留在家裡嗎？」

伊凡答道：「當然，你想待多久都可以，別見外。」

接著，伊凡坐下了來，二嫂卻面露嫌惡，説：「這麼臭的一個農夫，我沒辦法和他一起吃飯。」

泰瑞斯便説：「伊凡，二嫂沒法和你一起同桌吃飯，你自個兒去陽台那裡吃吧。」

伊凡回答：「好吧，反正我等一下就要去餵馬了。」

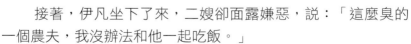

p. 74–75 解決泰瑞斯的那個小鬼來到了伊凡的農田,他四處找他的兩個好兄弟,但沒找著,只見到地上的兩個洞。

當天稍晚,伊凡走進樹林子裡伐木,他想建兩棟房子,分別給兩個哥哥住。

小鬼讓樹幹變得很硬,伊凡平常一天能伐五十棵樹,但今天樹幹太硬,只砍伐了十棵。伊凡坐了下來,累得筋疲力竭。

小鬼躲在高高的樹上,觀察伊凡的舉動。

「伊凡累壞了,沒辦法繼續砍樹,他們兄弟要是同住在一個屋簷下,一定會吵起來的。」

小鬼很得意,在樹枝上就手舞足蹈起來,未察伊凡已經起身,正對準小鬼藏身的樹,舉起斧頭用力砍了下去。

小鬼沒來得逃,樹就應聲倒下。小鬼從樹上摔下來,被伊凡給逮個正著。

p. 76 「這是什麼東西?」伊凡喊道:「我以為你已經走了!」

「我是另外一個啦!」

伊凡說:「那也不重要啦,反正我要用斧頭砍了你。」

「求求你,不要殺我!」小鬼哭喊道:「我可以製造黃金給你。」

「讓我看看你是怎麼做的。」伊凡說。

小鬼要伊凡去摘來一棵特殊橡樹的葉子,教他把葉子放在手上摩擦,當小鬼唸了幾句咒語後,葉子就全變成了金幣!

伊凡說:「這把戲真神奇啊,村裡頭的小孩子會很喜歡的。」

「那現在請讓我走吧。」小鬼懇求道。

「上帝保佑你!你可以走了!」伊凡說。

就在伊凡說出上帝兩個字時,小鬼也遁入了地下。

p. 78 伊凡很快就蓋好了兩個哥哥們的房子。田裡的工作完成後，他打算辦個宴席，邀請哥哥們來參加，但哥哥們都拒絕了他。不過，伊凡還是邀請了全村民，辦了一場宴會。他想讓大家都開心。

伊凡就重金邀請村中女孩唱歌。唱完歌後，女孩們向伊凡要酬勞。

「我這就去拿來。」伊凡於是走進森林，女孩們一面嘲笑著他。沒多久，伊凡就帶著一個大袋子走回來。他從袋子裡掏出許多金幣，灑向空中。

村民們很驚訝，開始爭著搶地上的金幣，這下子換伊凡嘲笑他們了。

伊凡笑嘻嘻地對小孩子們説，他可以叫士兵來為他們獻唱。於是他走進穀倉，領著一群士兵出來。士兵歌聲優美，大家聽得好不驚訝。

[第三章] 領袖伊凡

p. 82–83 第二天早上，西門來敲伊凡的門。

「弟弟，告訴我那些士兵是哪裡來的。」西門問道。

伊凡回答：「我這就告訴你。」他帶西門走進穀倉，用稻草做了一些士兵。

「這太神奇了！」西門説：「有了這樣的士兵，我就可以征服任何一個國家了！」

伊凡聽了很訝異：「早知道你之前就要來問我的，不過你必須保證把他們帶離這裡，我們沒有足夠的糧食供他們吃。」

西門允諾了伊凡，伊凡便為他做了一支龐大的軍隊。最後，西門好不容易終於喊道：「夠了，夠了。謝謝你，伊凡！」

伊凡答道：「這沒什麼，如果你還要軍隊，就再回來吧！」之後，西門便帶著軍隊離開，去攻打鄰近的國家了。

p. 84 西門一離開，換泰瑞斯來到伊凡的家。

他說道：「親愛的弟弟，告訴我你的黃金是從哪裡來的，只要我有一點錢，我就能夠成為一個成功的商人。」

伊凡驚訝道：「那你應該早一點告訴我的，跟我來吧。」

他製造了一堆的黃金，問泰瑞斯夠不夠。

「謝謝你，伊凡。」泰瑞斯說：「現在這些就夠了。」

伊凡回答：「如果你還有需要就回來，這一點也不麻煩。」於是泰瑞斯帶著他的黃金離開，去開創他的事業。

p. 86 如此一來，西門成了鄰近國家的統治者，泰瑞斯變成一名富商。只不過，他們仍不滿足。

「我沒有足夠的錢養兵。」西門說。

「我沒有足夠的士兵來看管我的錢。」泰瑞斯說。

「我們回去找伊凡吧。」西門說。

未料伊凡拒絕了他們：「西門，我不知道你的士兵會殺那麼多人！泰瑞斯，你把村子裡的母牛都買走了，村民又不能吃黃金過日子，現在都缺糧了！我後悔之前幫了你們。」

於是兩兄弟便離開，他們想到了一個新辦法。西門說：「我派一些士兵給你，你撥一些錢給我。」泰瑞斯表示同意，兩人遂都成了領主。

137

其間，伊凡拜他的本事和好心腸所賜，變得廣受歡迎，這塊領土內的人們，就選了他當領主。

p. 88 　魔鬼一直沒有聽到三個小鬼的消息，於是前來附近察看，卻看到三個兄弟都過得稱心如意。魔鬼看了大為光火，他決定要親自出馬，毀掉這三兄弟。

　　首先，他偽裝成大將軍前往西門家，教導他壯大自己的軍隊，還說他足以打敗印度。

　　於是，西門的大軍旋即再次征戰印度。然而，西門有所不知，魔鬼給了印度國王一種能夠飛行的機器，能對西門的軍隊空投炸彈。

　　西門無計反擊，打輸了這場戰役。他全軍覆沒，只得再一次潰逃。

p. 91 　接下來，魔鬼偽裝成一個富商，前往泰瑞斯的領地，高價買下所有物品，所以很快地，大家都想把自己的商品賣給魔鬼。

　　一開始，泰瑞斯樂見此事，因為這樣他就可收到更多的稅金。但之後他才發現到，自己已經買東西無門了。商人們為了賺更多錢，都把貨物賣給了魔鬼。一旦泰瑞斯開出更高的價錢，魔鬼也跟著提高買價。

　　過沒多久，只剩這商人支付泰瑞斯稅金。泰瑞斯光有一大堆黃金，卻買不到食物，最後餓得只得出走。

p. 92-93 　最後，魔鬼來到伊凡的領地。他看到那裡的人民工作辛勤，卻沒能存有什麼黃金，不過足以糊口而已。

　　魔鬼裝扮成將軍的模樣，來到伊凡面前，說道：「伊凡，你應該要有一個軍隊，我可以把你的人民訓練成強兵悍將。」

伊凡回答：「好啊，不過你也要教會他們唱歌和跳舞。」

於是魔鬼鼓勵年輕人來從軍，並承諾會提供伏特加和質料絕佳的制服。

但年輕人只是大笑道：「伏特加，我們已經喝得夠多了，制服嘛，我們不需要。」

「要是不加入軍隊，是會被判死刑的。」魔鬼說。

「我們要是從軍了，還不是一樣會戰死？」年輕人回答。

魔鬼發怒道：「從軍不一定會戰死，但不從軍，就唯一死刑！」

年輕人去找伊凡，說道：「有一位將軍說，我們要是不加入你的軍隊，我們就會被你判死刑。」

伊凡大笑道：「你們不想從軍，就別去從軍了。」

p. 94 老魔鬼氣極敗壞，他跑去鄰國塔卡尼亞，和國王結識。

他告訴國王，伊凡的領地極為易攻，國王便決定攻之。

然而，當軍隊來到伊凡的領地時，人民不但不反抗，反而還備上食物和水。

軍隊稟告國王說：「我們不想再為你打仗了，這裡的人民友善又愛好和平，我們要和他們共同生活。」

塔卡尼亞國王莫可奈何，只好獨自返國。老魔鬼更是火大了，他對伊凡所使的詭計都失敗了。

p. 96–97 魔鬼決定再試一次。他假扮成貴族，來找伊凡說：「我想要傳授給你智慧。」

伊凡回答：「好啊，那你就和我們住在一起吧。」

第二天，魔鬼來到村子裡，說道：「百姓們啊，聽我說！蓋一棟房子給我，我會支付黃金給你們。」

139

村民看到閃閃發光的黃金，甚是訝異，便開始為魔鬼蓋房子。農夫們拿食物來換取黃金，人們又拿黃金來做婦女的珠寶，或是做兒童的玩具。黃金一下子就夠用了，大家也頓時就不再拿東西和貴族交換黃金了。

魔鬼很納悶。他去找了幾戶人家，要用黃金換取食物。

但人們說：「你拿別的東西來換，我們就跟你換，再不然，你就用上帝的名義來要求幫助，那我們也會給你一些東西。」

但魔鬼只有黃金，而且光是聽到「上帝」這兩個字就會受傷。

p. 98–99 最後，魔鬼來到伊凡家。他肚子很餓，伊凡就要他一道來用餐。

伊凡的妹妹把菜端上桌，然而在伊凡的國家裡，雙手因為工作而變得又粗又黑的人，才能先享用食物。一雙手又細又白的人，是沒有人會上菜給他們吃的，他們只能等著吃剩菜剩飯。

想當然耳，那位貴族的雙手正是又細又白，還留著一手長指甲。當伊凡的妹妹看到那雙手時，便推開了魔鬼。

伊凡說：「請別感到被冒犯了，這是我們國家的法律。」

貴族生氣地問道：「難道你以為人只能夠用手來工作嗎？你真是個傻子，有很多困難的工作是要用腦袋來完成的。」伊凡對這些話印象深刻。

魔鬼又對他說，他會教伊凡的人民如何用腦子工作。第二天，魔鬼爬上高塔，對著人們演說。很多村民跑來聽他演講，不過他們都聽得一頭霧水。

他們在等他用腦袋工作，但他卻只是站在那裡嘰哩呱啦地說話。

p. 100–101 最後，魔鬼餓得沒力氣，就從塔上跌了下來。在他跌下來時，他的腿被一條繩子給勾住，身體在半空中左右晃動，頭顱往塔牆撞來撞去的。

村民們說道：「終於！貴族用他的腦袋在工作了！」

伊凡見狀後，說道：「唉呀！這樣工作很辛苦耶！用頭去撞牆，倒不如讓雙手變得粗糙！」

這時，繩子一斷，魔鬼摔了下來，伊凡急忙跑過去，但卻看到一隻大魔鬼躺在地上。

「我的上帝啊！這是什麼東西啊？」伊凡說罷，魔鬼立刻消失，在地上留下了一個大洞。

至於伊凡，他不但還是活得好好的，而且還有很多人來歸順。他統治的國家有一條未曾改變的法令：一雙手因為工作而變得又粗又黑的人，必先享用食物。

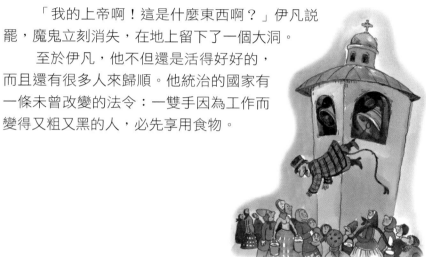

Answers

P. 28	**A** ① F ② F ③ T ④ T ⑤ T
	B ① left ② owed ③ spent ④ looked
P. 29	**C** ① -a ② -d ③ -b ④ -c
	D ① (c) ② (c)

P. 44	**A** ① -d ② -a ③ -b ④ -c ⑤ -f ⑥ -e
	B ① behind ② outside ③ inside ④ out of ⑤ from
P. 45	**C** ① → ③ → ②
	D ① (b) ② (c)

P. 62	**A** ① b c g ② a d e ③ f h
	B ① T ② T ③ F ④ F
P. 63	**C** ① (b) ② (c)
	D ① Simon hadn't worked on the farm.
	② The Devil had been disappointed to hear about Ivan.
	③ The pain in his stomach had gone away.

P. 80	**A** ① -c ② -a ③ -b ④ -d
	B ① -a ② -c ③ -b
P. 81	**C** ① After ② but ③ When ④ If ④ Before
	D ③ → ① → ② → ⑤ → ④

P. 102 **A** ❶ -d ❷ -b ❸ -e ❹ -c ❺ -a

B ❹ → ❷ → ❸ → ❶

P. 116 **A** **Martha** — ❶ She quickly gets angry, but a fair and kind person.
Tarras — ❷ He is a trader and likes to gather gold coins.
Ivan — ❸ He is a simple, honest and happy farmer.
The little devils — ❹ They are always making trouble for people.

B ❶ field ❷ dark, warm ❸ noticed ❹ pain

C ❶ Men who work hard with their hands have less problems than men who don't.
❷ People usually do not know when they are going to die.

P. 117 **D** ❶ Which sentence best describes the story, *Ivan the Fool?* (c)
❷ Which sentence best describes the story, *What Men Live By?* (a)

E ❶ The angel, Michael, disobeyed God.
❷ A woman died while giving birth to twins.
❸ Michael fell to the earth, naked and alone.
❹ Martha didn't like Michael at first.
❺ Michael saw the twins and learned the third truth.
❻ Michael made slippers for the rich gentleman.

❷ → ❶ → ❸ → ❹ → ❻ → ❺

托爾斯泰短篇小說【二版】
Short Stories of Leo Tolstoy

作者 _ 列夫・尼古拉耶維奇・托爾斯泰
　　　　（Lev Nikolayevich Tolstoy）
改寫 _ Brian J. Stuart
插圖 _ Ekaterina Andreeva
翻譯 / 編輯 _ 羅竹君
作者 / 故事簡介翻譯 _ 王采翎
校對 _ 賴祖兒
封面設計 _ 林書玉
排版 _ 葳豐/林書玉
播音員 _ Michael Yancey, Amy Lewis
製程管理 _ 洪巧玲
發行人 _ 周均亮
出版者 _ 寂天文化事業股份有限公司
電話 _ +886-2-2365-9739
傳真 _ +886-2-2365-9835
網址 _ www.icosmos.com.tw
讀者服務 _ onlineservice@icosmos.com.tw
出版日期 _ 2020年3月 二版一刷（250201）
郵撥帳號 _ 1998620-0 寂天文化事業股份有限公司

國家圖書館出版品預行編目資料

托爾斯泰短篇小說：人靠什麼活下去 / 傻子伊凡 /
Lev Nikolayevich Tolstoy 原著；Brian J. Stuart 改
寫 . -- 二版 . -- [臺北市]：寂天文化，2020.03
　　面；　　公分
ISBN 978-986-318-899-5(25K 平裝附光碟片)

1. 英語 2. 讀本
805.18　　　　　　　　　　　109002026